Jay Benson Hamilton

From the Pulpit to the Poorhouse

And Other Romances of the Methodist Itinerancy

Jay Benson Hamilton

From the Pulpit to the Poorhouse
And Other Romances of the Methodist Itinerancy

ISBN/EAN: 9783337044299

Printed in Europe, USA, Canada, Australia, Japan

Cover: Foto ©Andreas Hilbeck / pixelio.de

More available books at **www.hansebooks.com**

Jay Benson Hamilton.

FROM

THE PULPIT TO THE POOR-HOUSE

AND OTHER ROMANCES

OF THE

METHODIST ITINERANCY

BY

JAY BENSON HAMILTON, D.D.

NEW YORK: EATON & MAINS
CINCINNATI : CURTS & JENNINGS

DEDICATED TO MY FATHER,

REV. W. C. P. HAMILTON, A.M.,

A VETERAN

WHO ESCAPED SUPERANNUATION
BY SUDDEN TRANSLATION.

PREFACE.

"FROM THE PULPIT TO THE POOR-HOUSE" is a romance from real life. The line between fact and fiction can be drawn with difficulty by the author. It was first used as a sermon in the Trinity Methodist Episcopal Church, Providence, R. I. It was then rewritten and revised, and was used as an address at conventions and Annual Conferences. It awakened such deep interest that requests for its publication came from every part of the country. Many ministers solicited permission to use it as an aid in calling the attention of the Church to the needs of the veterans of Methodism. It now goes forth accompanied by other story-sermons of a kindred character. This attempt at preaching by "making believe" is a humble effort to imitate teaching by parable. If the thousands who may read will be as greatly interested as the thousands who have heard, no one will be more gratified than   THE AUTHOR.

CONTENTS.

FROM THE PULPIT TO THE POOR-HOUSE.

CHAPTER I.

A FATHER'S PURPOSE DEFEATED BY A MOTHER'S PRAYER.

"DON'T be a fool, John! You can't afford to throw your life away in the Methodist itinerancy. With the start I will give you, you can win success in any business or profession you choose. If you desire to be a farmer, here is the old homestead; it shall be yours. If you want to go to college and fit yourself for a profession, I will gladly help you. But to see you turn your back upon every opportunity for success to become a preacher among the poor and ignorant Methodists is the greatest grief of my life. If you will not listen to me now you will rue it to the end of your life."

"But, father—"

"Just wait until I am through, young man! I am an old fogy, I presume. The boys know more at twenty-five than the fathers do at fifty. You were going to say that to get money is not the worthiest object in life. I have heard you say that more than a hundred times. But you will find money is a handy thing to have around. That will be the first thing you will learn in the Methodist itinerancy. The itinerant is never tempted to get rich. God keeps him humble and the people manage to keep him poor."

"But, father—"

"I am not through yet. If you become a Methodist preacher you will spend your life in hard work and receive a bare support. As soon as you are worn out you will be cast adrift, like an old horse, to die. Your Church is not magnanimous enough to provide even a poor-house for its pauper ministers. A life of toil, privation, and sacrifice for the pittance of a common laborer! When ineffective because of gray hairs they will turn you adrift with scarce a crust. The pittance they will dole out to you will be as alms to a beggar and will be bestowed with such offensive parade that every instinct of manhood will forbid your accepting it unless you are reduced to absolute penury. If you select a profession with your ability and the training I will secure for you, you will at an early day secure an honorable position, obtain a competence and a home, and even in the decline of life you will receive your largest income. You will find your harvest-time at the very age when in the ministry you will be rejected and without either occupation, home, or means of support. If you decide to become a Methodist preacher you must do it with your eyes wide open. I have done my duty. I have only told you that which you as well as I know to be but the bare truth. What have you to say?"

"Father, I have decided to become a Methodist preacher if I have to die in the poor-house."

This brief dialogue occurred many years ago in a New England farm-house.* The father had little interest in or sympathy with religious people. In spite of his Methodist wife he claimed to have a positive dislike for, and bitter prejudice against, the Methodists. He was very proud of his bright, active boy, and was greatly vexed when the young man was converted and became a Methodist. When the father remonstrated, and threatened the son, he proved to be a chip of the old block. The father said one day:

"I have a great mind to turn you out of doors if you do not stay away from those pesky Methodists!"

The son quietly replied:

---

* When I read this story in New England I always located it out West. It saved trouble.

" Father, I have always honored and respected you ; but in this matter I claim the right to decide for myself. You have always urged me to have a mind and an opinion of my own. I have tried to obey you in other things and I demand the right to do so in my religion. I am a Methodist not from impulse, but from principle and conviction. If you bid me leave your house I will sorrowfully obey you ; but I cannot cease to be a Methodist."

The father was at first bitterly enraged, and then sorely grieved, when he learned that his son proposed to become a Methodist preacher. He tried every expedient to avert what he firmly believed would be a disaster. The morning that the young man was to start to the Annual Conference to be received on trial, the conversation took place which I have related at the opening of my story. When the father found all his arguments and entreaties of no avail he gave the young man the best horse in his barn, with bridle, saddle, and saddle-bags. He said, with a grim smile, as he noticed the surprise created by the very appropriate gift :

" I had reason to believe that you inherited enough of the family stubbornness not to heed your father's counsel. I have all along felt sure that you would persist in making a fool of yourself in spite of all my remonstrance and advice. I am not sure but I am largely responsible for your folly. ' Forbid a fool a thing and that he'll do.' If I had only remembered that ' fools are not to be convinced,' and had humored your fancy instead of opposing it, I might have saved myself the humiliation and you the misfortune of the blunder of this hour. If you will not listen to reason, but are determined to become a traveling beggar, my family pride compels me to give you a respectable outfit."

The young man, with tearful eyes, grasped his father's hard hand with a fervent grip and said :

" Father, I deeply regret that duty compels me to cause you so great a disappointment. I thank you for your generous gift." And then, with a smile through his tears, he said :

" I will try to prove false the old adage you have uttered so often : ' Put a beggar on horseback and he'll ride to the devil !' "

Mother and son had a tender parting upon which we will not intrude. The young man mounted his horse with wet eyes. That scene in his mother's chamber he would never forget. He had received his mother's farewell kiss and blessing. Her farewell words encouraged him as he thought about them all

the way to the Conference.   She had said, with eyes
shining through her tears :

"My son, I have prayed that you might become a
Methodist minister ever since the day you were born.
May God make you a successful one, is your mother's
only wish and prayer."

CHAPTER II.

A BITTER-SWEET HONEY-MOON.

IT will be impossible in this brief space to follow
the steps of the young itinerant through his whole
ministerial life.   Our purpose will be accomplished
by recording its closing chapters.   His experience was
in no particular different from that of most of his
brethren.   He began with the smallest and hardest
places.   His work was fairly successful, but required
the sacrifice and heroism so common to all itinerants as
never to receive mention.   His life passed unevent-
fully along year by year ; he rarely suffered from
want ; he never enjoyed the luxuries of life ; he was
always poor.   A brief glance at one of the many ap-
pointments he served may account for the smallness
of his savings.   The trip from the seat of Conference
to one of his charges was his marriage tour.   The

minister and his new wife, whose honey-moon began with the Conference session, had talked in a confidential way about the happiness of love in a cottage parsonage. They had tried to guess the shape and color of the house, the number of the rooms, and the pattern of the carpets and the kind of furniture until they had become so interested that each chided the other with preparing the way for a great disappointment.

They were met at the depot by a committee of a half-dozen of the leading members of the church. After the greeting was given, one after another began to say how happy they would be to have their new pastor and his wife stop with them ; but one "had such a small house ; " another "had a sick wife ; " another "had so many children." The minister said :

"Have you a hotel here ? "

"Yes," said one of the committee, who had not spoken ; " I keep the hotel ! "

" Please take our checks and have our baggage taken to the hotel. We will stop with you until we can make other arrangements."

This proposition was so quickly assented to by all as "just the thing," that the pastor and his wife said to each other, at the first moment of privacy, " That must have been arranged beforehand."

One week's boarding at regular hotel rates convinced

the minister that the small salary he was likely to receive would all be exhausted before the first quarterly meeting. "The parsonage is a little out of repair," the hotel-keeper said, a little testily, when he found he was to lose his boarders. He had insisted that, as business was business, the pastor should pay full price and weekly in advance. When the minister ventured to ask if the parsonage could not be sufficiently repaired to make it habitable the reply was still more curt:

"The church is too poor to repair it. There is no furniture, and the Ladies' Aid Society is too small and weak to buy any."

The minister and his wife visited the parsonage. It had not been opened for nearly a year. The former minister had been a single man, and the church had been unable to rent the house by reason of its dilapidated condition. It was a little cottage one story and a half high. The red paint with which it had been painted many years before had peeled off in many places and had faded in others, so that the question as to color was decided a draw. The wife suggested that "mottle" was the nearest color. It was situated upon a narrow back street. The gate was off the hinges; most of the fence was torn down; the yard had been the village resort for boys and wandering animals, until it was a sorry and desolate looking spot. The window sashes evidenced that the boys emulated the Benjamite accomplishment of slinging stones "at a hair-breadth without a miss." The porch swayed and creaked when the minister stepped upon it. After unlocking the door it required two men to force it open. The ceilings were low, black, and damp-looking; the walls had been papered, but much of the paper had fallen off; the floor was sunken and wet. The cellar was half full of water. The air felt damp and chill. Every thing was cheerless enough, but the wife said, with a bright smile through her tears :

"We have love and the cottage, you know."

The hotel-keeper, who had looked the house over with illy concealed disgust and contempt, said :

"I would not stable my horses in such a hole. If you prefer to go to housekeeping here, rather than board with me, you may. But you may be sure the church has no money to throw away fixing it up or furnishing it."

The pastor quietly replied :

"I have estimated the expense of boarding with you at the rate with which we have begun, and I find that the salary which has been estimated will pay our board with you just six months and leave us not a penny for clothes. I agree with you that this shanty is not fit for a decent stable ; but as it is the best our

2

people seem to care to do for a house for us we must make the best of it."

After a week's hard work painting, scrubbing, and papering, the old house began to look cosy and neat. Most of the wife's savings from her salary as a school-teacher were expended in very scantily furnishing two or three of the rooms. The first night they occupied their new home it rained. They were awakened by the dash of the rain upon the window and roof. The wife said:

"My dear, what a comfort it is to have a roof over our heads such a night as this."

Just at that moment a large drop of water fell in her face, followed in quick succession by a dozen small ones. The roof had sprung a leak. The water collecting over-head began to ooze through the plastering. She did not finish her remark. They moved the bed to another part of the room, but had scarcely lain down before a large drop fell in the minister's face. They moved the bed five times, and placed it under a leak every time. The minister tried to light a match, but the matches had been under a leak, too. After a long and blunder-ing search in the dark the minister found the umbrella, which he hoisted over their heads, saying:

"What a comfort it is, my dear, to have a roof over our heads such a night as this."

The night ended, as all nights must, but seemed in no hurry about it. The minister said, as daylight began to appear :

"Thank heaven, it's over at last."

He sprang back into bed with a cry of surprise and dismay. The water in the room was about ankle deep. The water from the hill back of the house, added to what came in through the roof, made a respectable sized pond for a family of two. The fire was out, the matches were wet, their clothes were thoroughly saturated with water, and the minister's boots were half full of water.

The parsonage was a fair illustration of the church. One incident of many of a similar character may give a faint idea of the broad-minded and liberal spirit of the officiary of the church.

One of the stewards brought in a fine turkey and a pumpkin pie as his usual Thanksgiving present to his pastor. The present was thankfully received. The minister, surprised out of his usual self-possession by the novelty of receiving a present of real value, said :

"This is such a large and fine bird it is a pity we have but two in our family; suppose you come and help eat it."

To the utter dismay of the minister and his wife,

the good brother instantly accepted the invitation, and said:

"I will bring my wife and all the family, so you won't be so lonesome."

When he had gone, the minister, seeing the look of sorrowful perplexity upon his wife's face, said:

"My dear, I was only joking; I had no idea he would accept."

She deliberately went to the book-case, and taking down the Discipline turned to rule second for a preacher's conduct, and read aloud: "'Be serious, avoid all lightness, jesting, and foolish talking.' My dear, please never joke again with that brother."

When Thanksgiving came the steward and stewardess and seven young stewards came. They ate as if they had fasted a week in anticipation of such a feast. When the next quarterly meeting came round the minister was handed by the church treasurer a bill for three dollars for the turkey. It was credited as one year's quarterage of the steward and charged as cash upon the pastor's salary.

"Let me see," said the minister; "how much did that turkey weigh?"

"Fifteen pounds."

"What is turkey worth a pound?"

"Fifteen cents."

"Then the turkey was worth two dollars and twenty-cents. That makes the pumpkin pie cost me seventy-five cents. The turkey is all right, but pumpkin pies are too great luxuries and a little too expensive for a family as large as ours at Thanksgiving."

CHAPTER III.

THE DONATION PARTY.

FOR three months the pastor had received but $5. He gently reminded the treasurer that funds were low. He had not money enough to buy a postage stamp. He wished to send a letter to the presiding elder. His credit was getting low. He had been dunned two or three times by the members of the official board with whom he had run an account for his necessary living. Some one suggested a donation party. The idea took. The cheerful occasion is best described by the victim himself. The account was not published in *The Christian Advocate;* we obtained it from the presiding elder. Here it is:

"DEAR BROTHER: We have had a donation. I have read of donation parties as painted in glowing colors by grateful recipients of overwhelming bounty.

When I read the newspaper reports, how I envied the pastors who had been 'pounded' and 'silvered,' and I wondered why I had been deprived of this delightful experience. I have no longer been deprived. I wish I had been. Our donation did not quite come up to my ideal. But then this is my first. I may get used to them in time. I wanted to mail you a letter, but had not money enough to buy a stamp. I gently hinted to our treasurer that money was scarce. I asked him if there was money enough in the treasury to send a letter to the presiding elder. He soberly replied, 'No; but I think there is enough to send a postal card. We are getting you up a donation, and then you will be all right.'

"Turkeys, chickens, hams, barrels of flour, suits of clothes, and purses of money in kaleidoscope form passed before my eyes continually. They haunted me with tantalizing day-dreams and gave me the nightmare at night. The day I first heard about it I hurried home. I threw my hat in one corner of the room and my overcoat in the other. I took my little wife in my arms and danced her all around the room, Sunday as it was. She wanted to know if I was crazy; if I knew what day it was. I said :

"'We are to have a donation. I will have a new suit of clothes. You will have a new dress. We will have a purse full of money. Our people do appreciate us after all.'

"I felt a little hurt that she seemed to take it so coolly, and asked her if she was not glad. She said she would wait until it was over before she expressed her opinion.

"I went to the market and bought—on credit, for I had no money—what I thought we would need to provide entertainment for those who might come. My wife worked late and early until she was all worn out and ready to go to bed with a sick headache. Despite her weariness and my dread of the debt incurred we both took great pride in the result of her labors. Chickens roasted, hams boiled, pies and cakes without number. Toward evening of the fateful day a committee of ladies came in and said we were to turn the house over to them. We did. The people came flocking in until the house was filled to overflowing. The old ladies were a little inquisitive and the young people were a little boisterous. But I consoled myself with the thought that donations do not come every day. A royal feast was spread. I was a little anxious when I saw there was nothing upon the table but what we had prepared. I was too excited and my wife was too ill to eat. But such appetites as our dear people had ! My wife's cooking

was complimented in the most flattering terms. One
good brother said : ' One look at this table ought to set
at rest forever all insinuations that we do not treat
our minister well. A man who can entertain his
friends with such a feast as this is remarkably well
provided for. My dear brother, you are to be con-
gratulated.'

"After supper the Sunday-school superintendent
made a very pleasant little speech, and in the name
of my many friends in the church and community
presented me with an envelope containing a sum of
money. It was too much for me. My self-command
failed me, and I wept. In a few broken words I expressed my thanks.

"We were soon alone. My wife desired to retire at
once, but I insisted upon seeing what presents we had
received. We went to the dining-room and found the
table covered with the fragments that remained of
our royal feast that were not trampled upon the
floor. The dishes were unwashed and piled in a
heap. We went into the pantry. All the chickens,
pies, and cakes my wife had prepared had disappeared.
In their place I found one pumpkin, a plate of dough-
nuts, and one mouldy mince-pie. We went to the
cellar and found one peck of small potatoes and one
more pumpkin, which the boys had marred a little by

using as a foot-ball. We went into my study. I found upon the back of my study-chair a cotton dressing-gown of bright colors and flaring figure. It was big enough for both of us. On my desk was a pair of carpet slippers, a little large and a little worn, and one flannel pen-wiper. My gold pen was gone. We went into the chamber. We found one small cotton handkerchief, a little soiled, four rolling-pins (old ones), and three potato-mashers (old ones). We went into the parlor. Our large parlor lamp was broken and the oil was all over the carpet. A walnut center-table was tipped over and one leg was broken off. The mirror was cracked, and a choice picture was soiled with dirty finger-marks. Three valuable books, soiled and badly torn, were lying on the floor. I remembered the young folks had been playing 'Copenhagen.' I was angry and clenched my hand, and found the envelope which I had forgotten. I opened it and found $1.32. The first glance showed one counterfeit quarter and one that was plugged. When I remembered how I had wept I was hardly able to control myself. To make things seem more aggravating, I remembered that after they had tired themselves out playing 'Copenhagen' they sang, 'There is rest for the weary.' I hoped at the time it betokened religious interest, now I was sure it was because there was nothing more to eat and no more deviltry they could perpetrate. The next day my treasurer waited upon me and presented me with a paper headed,

ACCOUNT OF DONATION.

REV. MR. ——— TO CHURCH TREASURER, DR.

Cash	$1 32
One dressing-gown	5 00
Two pumpkins	50
One pair slippers	75
Four rolling-pins	1 00
Three potato-mashers	75
One handkerchief	25
One peck of potatoes	25
One plate of doughnuts	15
One mince-pie	20
One pen-wiper	5
Services of ladies	5 00
Total	$14 22

" This was credited on my salary as so much cash.

" I prepared a sermon from the text : ' I was a-hungered, and ye gave me no meat: I was thirsty, and ye gave me no drink : I was a stranger, and ye took me in : naked, and ye clothed me not.' My wife found the manuscript and burned it. I am glad of it now, but writing the sermon relieved me. I desire to move next Conference—sooner, if possible."

CHAPTER IV

BEHOLD, THOU ART OLD.

OUR hero was a man of but ordinary parts. He was not learned or eloquent. He never was called to a great pulpit. He was an earnest, practical, faithful minister of the Gospel. He left every church better than he found it. He was instrumental in the conversion of many souls. He married a devoted Christian lady. God gave them several children. To his great consternation his meager salary did not increase as did his family. His income was always small. It was generally estimated, in accordance with the Discipline, at no more than enough for his support. Compelled to incur extra expense in dress, books, and papers, his receipts were about equal to the day-laborer. If by frugality and self-denial a little sum began to accumulate for a rainy day, sickness or pressing calls for charity soon extinguished it. Frequently the small salary estimated was partly paid in useless presents or undesired produce at exorbitant prices. As frequently, by the neglect or indifference of the stewards, a portion of the small salary was unpaid at the end of the year. These deficiencies were small sums in each year, but became a large amount in the aggregate as the years passed by.

The father of our hero after several years became reconciled to his son's choice of a profession. During a visit to his son he was converted and became an ardent Methodist. He became a generous giver to all church institutions. At his death, which occurred a few years after his conversion, he gave a large share of his modest fortune to the various benevolences of Methodism. The son's share of his father's estate was invested, at the suggestion of a friendly Methodist financier, in a silver mining company, and vanished when the bubble burst.

When the children began to incur the expense incidental to education many were the sacrifices required of parents and children to make both ends meet. Unkind remarks frequently reached the parsonage about the miserly disposition manifested by shabby attire and scanty patronage of the grocer. Lines in the pastor's brow and the white cheeks of the pastor's wife were the only signs that the gossip was heard. The only son who reached manhood sought to work his way through college. Too proud to make his wants known, he went thinly clad and poorly fed, and broke down before graduation. After a long illness the parents were broken-hearted to see in him their hopes extinguished. The only daughter who reached womanhood refused an offer of marriage from a worthy young man she loved, and upon the death of her brother put her young shoulder under the burden that was crushing her parents.

The Annual Conference which witnessed the twenty-fifth anniversary of our friend's entrance upon the ministry was an eventful one.

It was his birthday week as well. The presiding elder said to the bishop :

" I have no place upon my district for this man. He is a good preacher. He has been a successful minister. He has always left his churches in better condition than he found them. He is fifty years old; he is quite gray ; he is not as active as he once was ; his wife is in delicate health and cannot take an active interest in the parish work. I have tried to induce a number of churches upon my district to accept him, but all in vain. The cry is for young men. The young people are coming to the front in the management of the churches, and they demand youthful bloom, fire, and enthusiasm in the minister. Very few of them will consent to have an old man."

By exchange a place was found upon another district. He was sent to a remote country village church which had asked for a young man. They preferred

a single man, but would accept a married man without a family. The community was in a ferment
when they saw the gray-haired pastor and his almost
invalid wife. At first they threatened not to receive
him, but at last yielded to the presiding elder with
very poor grace. The salary was estimated at a sum
about enough for the support of a single man. The
expenses of the long move and the reduction in the
salary made the year one of pinching poverty. Both
pastor and people petitioned for a change at the end
of the year. The year was almost an utter failure.
Another place was found for the minister with great
difficulty. Again the church had asked for a young
man and received an old one.

CHAPTER V

A PAUPER PENSION FOR A VETERAN HERO.

TEN years passed with almost annual moves.
When the minister's sixtieth birthday arrived the
presiding elder said :

" My dear brother, I cannot carry you along any
further. You must superannuate. The other elders
cannot give you a place; I have none that will receive
you. If you will superannuate I will endeavor to

get you as large an appropriation from the fund for superannuated preachers as I can. If you do not superannuate I must request the Conference to locate you."

A series of resolutions very complimentary were unanimously adopted at the Annual Conference when our veteran requested to be superannuated. Several quite touching addresses were delivered. The bishop, with tears in his eyes, said:

"That is right, brethren, the wounded veteran, when no longer able for arduous service, ought to be retired to the hospital."

A small country village was selected for their home. Many years before they had spent two years with the people in very pleasant pastoral relations. The accumulated savings of the father and daughter were a few hundred dollars. A small cottage was purchased, partially paid for, and scantily furnished. Of course, we are unable to do more than glance in the briefest manner possible at this life now passing before us. An extract from a letter immediately after his superannuation may help us to a knowledge of how it feels to be superannuated.

To a young minister who wrote him a letter of sympathy upon his retirement he said:

"Dear Brother : I thank you from the bottom of

my heart for your kind and sympathizing words. My experience is much less sorrowful than that of many retired ministers. I am not entirely destitute and am still able to do a little work. But my heart is very heavy and the outlook is very dark. I am not disappointed. I have been looking forward to this for years. For all that, when the ' thud ' came it hurt worse than I thought it would. I am not able to take work, and yet without work I have nothing to live on. When I settled down in this little home, so scantily furnished, unfitted for any secular business, with no outlook for daily bread, I was greatly disheartened. When I saw my dear old wife, all the more dear because she was old, unpack our goods and begin to get ready for housekeeping, how my heart ached! When I remembered that I had no church, no Sunday-school, no prayer-meeting, no work, no income, it was more bitter than death. You can never anticipate it."

To an aged brother who had been his presiding elder, but who was now, like himself, superannuated, he wrote a brief letter, explaining why he had retired. He said:

" Dear Brother : The saddest day of a Methodist minister's life has arrived for me. I did not desire to superannuate, but was constrained to do so to relieve the embarrassment of the appointing powers. How

I am to live one year without any income, the dear
Lord only knows.   It seems to me as if there was a
mistake in our economy.   When a minister is unable
to preach he ought to die.   It would be a fitting
ending to his ministry were he to preach his farewell
sermon with his own empty coffin just before him.
When his sermon was ended he should lie down in
his coffin and be carried out and buried.   He should
cease at once to work and live, and go home to receive his crown."

To this letter the ex-presiding elder replied:

" DEAR BROTHER : The distressing feature of your
case is, there is nothing unusual about it.   It is the
common lot of the old men of the Church.   When I
was a presiding elder, one of our excellent bishops—one
of the best of them—speaking of the difficulties that
beset himself and colleagues in making the appoint-
ments, said to me: 'The venerable men who have
borne the burden and heat of the day have to be provided for, and the young men are kept out of appoint-
ments they feel themselves competent to fill and they
become restive.   Now, if some of these dear old brethren would consent to step aside and give their places
to the younger and more active men it would relieve
the embarrassment.'

" Indeed !   Where will they go?   Where are they
3

to live, and how? Will somebody tell? If there is a man in the Methodist Episcopal Church for whom there is no place it is the average superannuate. I have served in the cabinet with eight or nine of our bishops and know somewhat of the embarrassment that besets the appointing power at times; but I have never known any embarrassment like that which came upon me when I had to step aside. To have no place to go, nothing to depend on for a living, is, I find, very embarrassing."

What proved a very serious embarrassment to our hero, as to all like him, was, that the little allowance made him by the Conference was not due until the session of the next Conference. He had to make provision for one year's expenses without any income from the Church at all. When he made application for aid he was surprised and grieved to find himself compelled to submit to an examination intended to reveal to the committee his absolute penury. The basis of distribution was necessity and distress. He was made to feel that the amount to be received was not a pension, but a gratuity. His allowance was not in part the payment of a just debt, but a gift of charity extorted by his pathetic appeal. The following blank was forwarded to him for his signature:

Blank for Conference Claimants.

By action of the Conference the stewards are not permitted to allow any claim where answers to the following questions are refused. Every question must be answered.

1. Name and post-office address.
2. Number of years in effective ministry.
3. How long a superannuate.
4. Number and age of family dependent on you.
5. State of their health.
6. Income from their labor.
7. Income from your own labor.
8. Value of property, house and lot, real estate, notes, and other items.
9. Total net income on the above.
10. What donation or aids from friends other than these.

We send you two blanks. Fill them both. Send one to your next Quarterly Conference and the other to the Secretary of the Conference Stewards. To no one else, to avoid trouble.

This was received and read aloud by the old minister with trembling voice. After a moment's silence he bowed his head in his hands and burst into tears. Then, nervously walking the floor, he cried:

"Has it come to this? If I were able to earn bread and fuel without it I would not take it. Are we paupers, wife, dear? Is this relief extended us charity, or is it a beggarly part payment of a just debt?"

Driven by absolute need to fill out the blank, it was blotted with tears when finally signed. For once the brave little woman had no comfort to give. Her eyes were too bright for tears. She said, quietly, but with an emphasis very unusual for her :

"It is dishonorable to the Church and unjust to you and your fellow-laborers. It is a humiliation to which we must submit; we cannot help ourselves; let us not talk about it any more, except to our Father. He will make it all right when we get home."

The allowance was but $100, because the blank showed that the superannuate owned a house and lot worth $800, which was mortgaged for $500.

The community did not seem pleased at the return of the old pastor. Most of those who had known him were dead or had moved away. Some of the people were ungenerous enough to say that the old man had come back to be supported. The new pastor was a very young man, and was ambitious to be the sole pastor of the parish. He disliked to share with another the pleasant duties of ministering to the people at the sacramental table, at baptisms, weddings, and funerals. The presence of a former pastor, who was continually reviving old memories of happy incidents of pastoral relations, was very irksome and embarrassing. The keen eyes and ears of the old minister soon discovered the condition of things, and he kindly relieved the embarrassment by declining nearly all such invitations. This was attributed to jealousy and sourness, and created a coldness and indifference toward him in the minds of the members of the church.

A severe and protracted illness robbed the home of the labor of the daughter's hands. By canvassing for books the old minister had succeeded, with his daughter's aid, in barely supporting his family. Several months' illness of the daughter and increasing infirmity of the father cut off all income. An appeal was made to the Conference, and the allowance was increased $25. At last the daughter died. The interest of the mortgage upon the house could not be paid, and the mortgage itself was increased by borrowing small sums of money to relieve immediate distress. At last the old people became objects of charity. The needs were frequent and urgent, until the patience of the people became exhausted.

CHAPTER VI.

VIVISECTING THE VETERAN.

THE Ladies' Circle was in session. A casual in-
quiry concerning the health of the old minister's wife led to a conversation very general and
pointed. One sister, very active in the Woman's
Foreign Missionary Society, said:

"I think it is too bad that this old minister should
be left upon our hands to be supported. When I
solicit money for foreign missions I am reminded
that charity begins at home. The people plead that
they are continually giving to the poor at home, and
especially to the poor old minister. I hoped to
raise one hundred dollars for our Missionary Society,
but fear it will be hard work."

Another lady, active in the Woman's Christian
Temperance Union, said:

"This very family embarrasses me in my work.
I have been soliciting clothing and shoes and money
to relieve the distress of the families of the intem-
perate in our town and the people are continually
saying, 'You had better relieve the distress of the
old minister.' I declare, I am tired hearing his
name."

Another lady, who had just assisted in organizing a Woman's Home Missionary Society, said:

"It is a little strange, but I find myself embarrassed in the same way by the same family. I have been soliciting aid for the neglected and suffering freedmen of the South, and many have replied, 'Had you not better relieve the neglected and suffering minister's family?' I believe I would rather go to the poor-house than become a burden to my friends and a nuisance in the community.

CHAPTER VII.

ST. MICHAEL THE RAVEN.

THE day the Ladies' Sewing Circle met was cold and raw. The old minister and his wife sat together in the little kitchen by their only fire. He was pretending to read the Bible which lay open upon his knee; she was pretending to patch a worn garment. Both watched each other with stolen glances, as if waiting for the first word. The old man shivered with the cold, and mechanically arose to replenish the fuel in the stove. He took the empty hod and started toward the door. He opened the door and then suddenly stopped, turned, and, closing the door, he replaced the hod and sat down by his wife. He gently took her hand, and said, softly:

"I had forgotten that I had scraped the coal-bin before. Do you suppose the coal-man has forgotten the order? I wonder why the grocer has not sent the tea and sugar and flour I ordered this morning? Have you any thing for supper, wife, dear?"

She made no reply, but simply shook her head. He continued:

"I must go and see about the coal and groceries before it gets dark."

The coal merchant was not in his office; but a pert boy of ten years of age seemed to be in charge. He said:

"Father told Mike he need not mind about taking up your coal. You had not paid for the last load yet. May be if you'd get pretty well chilled you'd settle. Do you want to pay for the last load now? If you do, I'll send another load right away."

"My son, I cannot pay you any money to-night; you need not send any coal."

At the grocer's the clerk spoke a little sharply. "Your bill is more than a month behind, and I was told not to fill any more orders without the cash."

With a heavy sigh the old minister said:

"I cannot pay you any thing to-night."

He seemed to try to make the journey between the store and his house as long as possible. His usual slow step now dragged, but in spite of him his own door soon opened to his tardy feet.

He seated himself by the stove, now growing cold, and for a moment said nothing. Very slowly and softly he said :

"Wife, dear, it is what I feared and yet dreaded to know. Neither coal nor groceries have been sent because they feared they would not be paid for."

Almost whispered came the answer :

"I knew it would be so."

He took her hand gently, and, tenderly stroking it, said :

"Never mind, wifey, dear, the dear Lord has a long bank account. He can provide for the coal and the grocer's bill. He can order new supplies, if it is best. If it is not, it won't matter. It will only hasten a little our summons home. We will trust him all the same. Wife, dear, I have never begged. I would die before I would do it for myself; but for you I will do any thing. The honor of our dear old Church is at stake. For a worn-out minister to beg for food and fuel would be a terrible disgrace. I am not sure but it will be better for us to do what they wish. If it were not for you, I would gladly die before I should

go to the poor-house.   But for you who have been my
comfort and my good angel all our married life I
will do any thing or go anywhere.   How the enemies
of dear old Methodism would rejoice to know that an
aged minister and his wife had become the inmates
of the poor-house through neglect of the Church to
provide for them in their helpless old age.   Wife, dear,
for your sake I will submit to this indignity even at
the expense of the honor of my Church which I love
dearer than life, but not dearer than you."

"No, husband, dear," the wife replied; "I love my
Church too much to become a reproach to her.   I
honor you too much to consent that for my sake you
shall dishonor yourself and Methodism by becoming
a town's pauper.   Honest poverty is no shame; but
the many years of arduous, illy paid labor of our lives
creates a debt of honor.   The Church cannot ignore
it without grave wrong.   I would rather die than
have you become the object of charity because of unfaithfulness or neglect of duty.   We have been faithful; we cannot degrade ourselves by announcing that
we are receiving a fair recompense for service.   We
cannot shame or dishonor our Church by publishing
her unfaithfulness.   It will be better and easier to die."

This little speech was punctuated by tears and sobs
which almost broke the old man's heart.   He sank

upon his knees, and, clasping both of his wife's hands
in his, he drew her head to his shoulder and began
to pray. He was not gifted in speech, but was
known among his brethren as eloquent and mighty in
prayer. The old fire returned; he prayed as he had
prayed in his youthful ministry. Always sweet, trust-
ful, and tender, yet burning with earnestness, buoyant
with faith, and joyful with hope, he talked with God.

A man without stood with his hand on the door.
He had been an unconscious listener to both conversation and prayer. Through the partially drawn
blinds he had witnessed the old pair kneeling in each
other's arms. As the prayer began he took off his
hat. The tears soon began to flow. He wiped them
away with the sleeve of his coat, and when the prayer
ended he sobbed out, "Amen!" in regular old Methodist fashion.

"Father Maginnis may call the Methodist praist a
herrytick, but, faith, he prays like a saint. He looks
like an old prophet. Oim a purthy lookin' bird to
come a fadin' the old prophet; raven, is it? More
like a crow; sure, oim black enough for ayther,"
looking at his hands grimed with coal-dust.

A deep silence followed the prayer. The old people were both upon their knees when they were
startled by a loud knock. Before they could open

the door, Mike, the coal-driver, staggered in. He had a bag of coal on his back and a basket on his arm. Placing the coal by the stove and the basket upon the table, he said:

"The blissed book says, God sint a blackbird to fade a praist, and here he is."

The old people looked at him and began to smile. The tears had plowed their way down Mike's cheeks through the black grime, and his face shone through in great white streaks and blotches. Mike looked in the mirror and roared with laughter at his comical appearance. Checking himself, he took off his cap and made a profound bow.

"Your riverence, I heard that young shalpane givin' yez some sass about your coal-bill. The loikes of it, ez if it wern't honor enough for yez to burn his miserable old coal widout payin' for it. An' I followed ye like a snake-thafe, dodgin' in the dark behind yez, and I heard that bloody-moinded thafe at the grocery insultin' ye. I sez to meself, sez I, 'The old praist sha'n't fraze this blissed night, if I have to sthale the coal.' An' mind yez, your riverence, I did sthale it. I sthole it from Bridget; that's my old woman, your riverence. An', if I do say it, she's the best woman the Lord iver made, barrin' the prisent company.' Sez Bridget, sez she, 'Mike, you thafe,

I've caught you this time. I've heard you a talkin' about the old praist bein' cold and hungry, an' I've stholen a few bits from the children. An' moind ye, don't ye sphill it or I'll break your black head,' sez she. That was a bit of plisantry, your riverence. I sez, sez I, 'Bridget, you're a darlin',' an' when I kissed her I made a black spot on her nose that would have made your riverence die a laughin' to see. May the Holy Vergen an' all the saints bliss you an' fade you an' kape you warm an' see you safe home to hivin, but not be in any too great **hurry** about movin' ye!"

He was gone. By the blazing fire a blessing was asked over the humble meal. The old minister said, looking at his wife:

"I knew our Father had coal and bread. It's just like him, isn't it?"

The official board of the church had assembled for their last meeting before the Annual Conference. The pastor was requested to urge a larger appropriation for the superannuated minister. One brother, who was one of the selectmen, said:

"You may as well say to the Conference stewards that if they do not provide for this old man's support he will be taken to the poor-house. We do not propose as a church to carry the burden any longer."

CHAPTER VIII.

BITTER AS DEATH.

THE Conference stewards were in session, considering the claims of the superannuated ministers. The session was a secret one, as it was deemed unwise to scandalize the Church by advertising the niggardliness of her dealing with her faithful servants. Reports were called for from the various applicants for aid. These were given in personal letters from the claimants themselves. We take a few as samples:

" The heathen and the freedmen have their eloquent pleaders. Who is there to plead for us? Anniversaries are held for every benevolence but the one which is the most important of all. How can God bless and prosper Methodism when she is so forgetful of those who laid the foundation of her greatness? I gave the Church my life and labored many years for a smaller salary than I could earn digging in the streets. I am now old, helpless, and in need. The small allowance permitted me has been wasted by sickness, until we have been in real want. For weeks at a time we have not had either milk, butter, or meat upon our table."

This brother really wanted his apportionment increased $25. The committee had to decrease it $20.

Another said:

"We have frequently been in circumstances of real poverty and depression, without food or means to purchase it. My wife cannot, when in health, go to church, because she has not suitable clothing. My only dependence is the aid from Conference. It is very painful to me to mention these things, and I would not had you not requested me."

Another brother, eighty-one years of age, who was living with his venerable wife in a little country place, wrote:

"I have obtained a part of my fuel by picking it up in farmers' woods, cutting and preparing it for the fire myself. We have dispensed with eating much fresh meat, and have lived among old friends that have been very kind. I have worn second-hand clothing, and in every way have tried to live cheaply; and by the help of a good wife have been happy and cheerful, and there are no clouds to darken the skies of my future home but a small distance ahead."

Another brother, eighty-four years of age, had an invalid wife and daughter to support. He said:

"I have been superannuated now nineteen years, and I have not been able to get myself a Sunday coat during all this time. I wear the same one I had while preaching. My every-day clothes are of the cheapest material, and I have been obliged to go through this past bitter winter with only a pair of shoes, not being able to purchase either boots or over-shoes."

A brother who had done faithful and effective service for forty-five years wrote:

"I have been humbled enough to beg. I have been so cold and hungry and sorrowful that I was obliged to, and the end is not yet."

Another brother wrote:

"I am seventy-seven years of age and in very poor health. I have no income but what my friends are pleased to give me. We have lived five years in damp basements, but hope to have the comfort of living above ground what little time we remain on earth."

Another wrote:

"I have been a Methodist minister in good and regular standing for over fifty years. I have been brought next door to the poor-house. I have not a woolen dresscoat or overcoat fit to wear in public. My wife said to me the other day if I should die soon or suddenly, which I am liable to do, being in my eighty-fourth year, they would have to get a coat to lay me out in. Somebody wrote a note for *The Christian Advocate* begging a coat for a poor old preacher. The coat came, but it was too small. I said to my wife, 'I guess I had better keep it. I won't mind the tight fit when I'm dead.'"

Another wrote:

"I am unable to go to church because my wardrobe is in ruins. I cannot go out when it is wet and keep my feet dry. I am in debt $100 for provisions and doctor's bills. My wife did the housework for our physician to pay for our board, but after four months she had to give up on account of sickness. We are now living on credit, with not a dollar on hand."

There were fifty claimants on the worn-out preachers' fund of the Conference. These fifty persons, all told, received an income of $1,341.67, aside from what the Conference was able to give them. Only thirty of the fifty had any property at all, and these thirty really received this income of $1,341.67, and it averaged among the thirty a trifle over $44 apiece. The other twenty persons had not a dollar of property in the world, and, being old and feeble, were not able to earn any thing; so that their entire support was the pittance from the Conference funds.

The claim of our hero was decreased instead of

4

increased. The collections did not meet the apportionments. When the news reached the old minister's home it caused an explosion. The owner of the mortgage waited upon the old man, and said:

"The mortgage on this house exceeds its value. I cannot let my money lie here without interest. You must look for another house at once."

"But where shall I go? My wife is almost helpless, and I am not much better."

"I do not know where you will go unless to the poor-house. Our selectmen say you cannot go to our poor-house, as you are not a resident of our town. You will be sent to the town where you were born."

CHAPTER IX.

ON THE ROAD TO THE POOR-HOUSE.

THE Ladies' Sewing Circle met at the parsonage. The old minister at once became the subject of the conversation. Several of the ladies had favored the proposition to remove the old people to the poor-house, and be rid of the burden. Others had strongly opposed it, and denounced it as a burning shame and disgrace.

The pastor's wife was a very young woman, and

had come to their parsonage but a few days before as a newly wedded bride. She listened attentively to the conversation. A moment's silence followed the very vigorous remark of one lady, that "paupers ought not to expect any thing better than the poor-house."

The pastor's wife slowly rose to her feet, her slight girlish form towering to its fullest height. Her face was snow-white, but her eyes were ablaze. All were startled to a deathly stillness by the strange tone of her voice as she asked, with great emphasis :

"I beg your pardon, ladies, but of whom are you talking ? "

A little hesitatingly, one lady said :

"Of the old superannuated minister, who for years has been a burden upon our church and community."

"Am I right in understanding that this old couple are to be taken to the poor-house ? "

"Yes," said another lady, as she dropped her eyes before the searching glance of the white questioner ; "my husband is one of the selectmen, and he told them to be ready to-day." Taking out her watch, she said : "He is about there now. They are to take the three o'clock train."

"Not while I have a shingle over my head or a crust in my house," said the minister's wife. "My father was a Methodist minister. He could not lie easy in his honored grave if I were to permit it. How can the people be so heartless! Excuse me, ladies, I am going there at once."

The circle broke up in great confusion. With scarce a word each lady hastened to her own home. Hurrying to her husband's study, the minister's wife told her story between her sobs. He listened in amazement.

"It cannot be. It must be a mistake. I noticed that he looked very sad and dispirited when I called upon him yesterday. But, being such a stranger, I hesitated about asking him the cause."

"Come and go with me, husband; I cannot wait. Perhaps we are too late now."

They hurried to the remote part of the village where the old minister lived. They saw the carriage of the selectman at the door. The old minister was just helping his feeble wife into the carriage as the minister and his wife reached the gate.

"This is very disagreeable business, dominie," said the selectman.

The young minister made no reply for an instant, as he sought to control his emotions. At length he said:

"Lend me your carriage a few minutes."

" Why, where are you going ? "

The young man assisted his wife into the carriage, and, taking the reins out of the selectman's hand, the minister simply said :

" To the parsonage. Good-day."

The amazed town official watched the rapidly departing vehicle for a moment, then, with a long, low whistle, turned, and, closing the door of the old minister's house, sent the key by a boy to the parsonage.

The whole town was aflame with indignation. Every sinner was thoroughly mad, and every saint was horribly ashamed. The promptness and boldness of the young minister had stirred every conscience. There was not a dissenting voice when Mike, sitting upon his coal-cart, shouted, as soon as he heard the news :

"Three chares for the young praist an' the young praisteȿs ! May they live foriver; but when they do die, may they go to the poor-house where the Holy Vergen is the overseer. But bad luck to the mane, dirty lunk-head that tried to make a pauper out of the old prophet. God bliss the old saint and fade him on the fat of the land."

CHAPTER X.

AN AQUA-FORTIS SERMON.

THE village paper announced that the subject of the sermon at the Methodist church next Sunday morning would be, "Shall we send our heroes to the poor-house?" A congregation was present that filled every inch of space. The text of the sermon was, "When I am old and gray-headed, O God, forsake me not" (Psa. 71. 18).

The preacher gave a brief sketch of the life of the old pastor, and then said:

"Thirty-five years have been given to self-denying and laborious service. Hundreds of souls have been converted through his ministry. A dozen churches are strong and well-to-do which he saved. This very church was in peril when he was its pastor. Of his poverty he gave as much as any of you. From his pastorate dates the beginning of your strength. For a pittance scarcely equal to the poorest toiler in your streets this man of God served you faithfully. What return have you made?

"You have been spared the crime of consummating a shameful and ungrateful act. Let us praise God for that!

"You have societies to send the Gospel to the heathen, to educate the freedmen, to minister to the families of the vicious poor in your own midst; have you done your whole duty by this sainted woman, this holy man? My cheek tingles with shame that my beloved Church in her days of strength and wealth doles out a miserable pittance to those who laid the foundation of her greatness. She ought to support these men and women as her first duty to God. Give none the less for the heathen, the freedmen, or the unfortunate, but as you hope to escape God's wrath do not neglect or cause to suffer his children, who gave up all chance for earthly honor or profit for the service of God. As a thank-offering for being prevented from sending these old saints to the poorhouse I want you to give one thousand dollars. This will pay for their little home, comfortably furnish it, and give them a small bank account."

The owner of the mortgage upon the old minister's home arose, and with trembling voice confessed his harshness, and said, as a partial atonement for what he saw was a mean and contemptible sin, he would wipe out all unpaid interest and give one hundred dollars.

The President of the Woman's Foreign Missionary Society spoke with deep emotion. She regretted that

she had been so absorbed in her delightful mission
that she had committed a grave wrong. "I have
only thought of the heathen in foreign lands and have
cared nothing for the needy saint next door. Our
society authorizes me to pledge one hundred dollars
as our share of this thank-offering."

The President of the Woman's Home Missionary
Society said :

"I have been thoughtless and wicked. I have seen
very clearly the black faces in the South-land but
have been blind to the white-haired hero and heroine
in my own home. Our society pledges one hundred
dollars."

The President of the Woman's Christian Temperance Union said, in a voice full of sobs :

"I have wept over the drunkard's family, but have
had no tears for the old minister in distress. I have
spoken bitterly of the saloon-keeper. Alas! I find I
have been as cruel as he, and still I have been cher-
ishing the hope that I was a Christian. Our society
wishes to pledge one hundred dollars as our share
of the thank-offering."

Pledges came in thick and fast, until the pastor,
lifting his hand, said :

"We have raised one thousand dollars, keep the
rest for another time."

" Hold on, your riverence. I'm not accustomed to shpakin' in matin', especially Mithodist matin's. But when I heard you was going to preach the risurrection sermon of the old praist I wanted a hand in the job. My own praist will make me do pinance for bein' here at all, but I'm under orders I'm afraid to disobey. Sez Bridget, sez she—Bridget is Mrs. Corrigan, your riverence, and I'm Mike Corrigan ; Bridget, she's my ould woman—sez Bridget, sez she, ' Mike, if yez'll go to the Mithodist matin' an' shpake a few words, I'll pray to the Vergen to be kind of aisy wid yez for the mortal sin. There's the money for the new gown I was goin' to git, an' there's the money for the chil- ders shoes—they can go barefoot this summer ; an' Mike,' sez she, wid a sly glance out of the corner of her eye, ' if you'll take the money you was goin' to shpend for the beer an' the pipe, shure it would make a dacint nist-egg for the ould praist.' I sez, ' Bridget,' sez I, ' my swate-heart, if yez can go widout your new gown an' the childer can go barefoot for the ould praist, I would be maner than a thavin' sphal- pane if I couldn't go widout my pipe an' beer ; an' ' I sez, sez I, ' I will touch nayther agin while the ould praist is hungry an' cold.' Sez Bridget, sez she, ' May the ould praist niver fraze or starve, but kape just cold an' hungry enough to decave you into kapin' your pledge.' When I told her for the ould praist's sake I would take the pledge for a hundred years, sez Bridget, sez she, ' Mike, your a blissid ould darlin',' an' she cried an' she laughed an' hugged me till I thought she'd break every bone in my body. I sez, sez I, ' Bridget, darlin', be aisy wid yez ; ye'll be afther huggin' me to death entirely.' An' at that she kissed me on the chake an' set my heart on fire, an' it is burnin' yet. I fale as if a daper work of grace or something afther that fashion was goin' on inside of me. Here's twinty dollars from Mike an' Bridget an' the childer. An', if yez'll not take offince at my liberty, I will close my fable remarks by axin' the audience to join me in three chares for the ould praist, an' a tiger for the ould lady."

Mike led off with three lusty shouts and most of the congregation joined him. His hearty tiger at the end was echoed by a hallelujah from the amen-corner that made even the minister smile.

For several years the old minister and his wife remained the loved and honored guests of every home, and finally were laid away to rest with tears from every eye in town.

CHAPTER XI.

FACTS MORE TERRIBLE THAN FICTION.

THE preceding story is a romance. It is therefore dismissed as unreal, because it is the invention of the imagination.

No novelist need invent a tale to melt the heart; he needs but to record the story of some real life. We give two life-stories, in brief, that need no romancer's art to make them tales of thrilling pathos.

Just one hundred years ago a lad of thirteen gave God his heart. An older brother had heard a sermon from an earnest Methodist preacher. His influence upon his young brother led him to Christ. The lad was early called to preach. Before he was twenty-one years of age he was licensed to exhort and the next year he was appointed a junior preacher upon a circuit which embraced six hundred miles of travel and more than sixty preaching places.

Among the fruits of his first year's labors was the conversion of a man who afterward became a Bishop of the Methodist Episcopal Church. The next year the young man was received into Conference and began a long itinerant career. He was received into full connection after two years' probation by one of the first Conferences in the Church, which has now grown to six great Conferences. The record says of him: " He is a faithful and useful preacher. After due examination he was unanimously voted into the connection and elected to the office of a deacon in our Church."

His itinerant life reads like an incredible romance. He had long rides over bad roads; he crossed rivers without ferry-boats; among his experiences were buffeting storms, breaking roads, sleeping in open cabins and log huts, with coarse and scanty fare. He threaded forests by marks upon the trees; his horse was dangerously lacerated in fording streams amid the ice; the stars shone upon him through the log-cabin in which he sought shelter. The total salary at this time of the twenty-two members of the Conference, of whom but four were married, was $2,206 ; the receipts were $1,518. Driven from the active work by inability to support his family he located ; but for twelve years did as much work without any salary as he had ever done while in the itinerancy. He re-entered the itinerancy and was three years a presiding elder.

After preaching five years he was again compelled to locate. After eight years trying to support his family and preach as a local preacher he again re-entered the itinerancy, and for twelve years more served the Church. He was compelled through the infirmities of age to superannuate after having given forty-four years to the ministry—twenty years without any salary, and twenty-four with the barest pittance. About the time this old minister superannuated a presiding elder in his Conference issued an appeal in the interest of superannuated preachers. A few quotations from this will give a fair idea of the condition of the class of ministers to which this veteran was retired :

" Many of these men are distressingly poor. They find it exceedingly difficult, if not impossible, to make their families comfortable without involving them in debt when there is little if any probability of paying. Their principal, if not entire, dependence is the scanty pittance paid them annually by the stewards, which, in most cases, is less than one fourth of the sum judged by the General Conference to be only sufficient to afford them a comfortable support."

"With you, brethren of the laity, are the means of affording relief from hunger and want and tears those whom Providence and the Church have cast upon you for support. The suppressed groan of the broken-down minister, the flowing tear of his distressed widow, the piercing cry of his hungry orphan all come up before God against you. 'Behold, the hire of the laborers who have reaped down your fields, which is of you kept back by fraud, crieth: and the cries of them which have reaped are entered into the ears of the Lord of Sabaoth.' Now, brethren, can you, will you, suffer those who have traversed your pathless forests, forded your bridgeless rivers and streams, sought you in your retired and humble cottages, and suffered with you from the pinching hand of hunger and want; will you, I inquire, suffer their sun to set in the dense cloud of poverty and want? Think on the days when in your poverty you cheerfully divided your last meal with them, so glad were you to have their counsels, instructions, and prayers in your families, and suffer them not to go hungry while you have enough and to spare. Is it now nothing to you that those who have spent their lives for you and yours until broken down and unable to do more should linger out their remaining miserable years in distress and want? Have you, brethren, no feelings of pity, if destitute of moral justice, to impel you to afford relief? According to the exhibit of the secretary of the Conference twelve cents from each of you will raise the needed sum."

Alas! that it must be recorded that, despite repeated

appeals as eloquent as this, the collections amounted to less than one cent per member.

After eighteen years of superannuation he died, leaving to an unmarried daughter the care of an invalid wife.   His small farm brought a few hundred dollars, and the Conference made the widow an allowance of $21.76 for the year ; which was as large a sum as was given to any claimant.   The widow died, and the daughter had the care of an invalid sister, for many years toiling to support her as well as care for her in her helplessness.   At last, after a life-time of hardest toil, this unmarried daughter found herself friendless, penniless, and almost helpless.   She was unable to work ; she was ashamed to beg.   She went to the authorities of the town where her father had re-tired as a superannuated minister and asked to be sent to the town farm.   There, within a few miles of the city where her father had helped found Methodism, where he had been a presiding elder for three years, in a circuit of churches in each of which her father had established the first class, she remained two years in the poor-house.

Some one sent her a bundle of Church papers. She found in the New York *Christian Advocate* an article from the author of this book. She wrote a letter to him, as the article requested, in which she said :

"I am not a veteran or a Conference claimant, yet I want to write you, hoping to receive a word of sympathy. After long years of suffering and hard work I was at last brought to the last resort—that of calling on the town ; so here I am at the town farm, a *pauper*, with the bright prospect of filling a pauper's grave. But there is a silver lining to this dark cloud : Christ is mine and a sweet assurance that when done with earth heaven is mine. If you will write me a letter full of sympathy and good advice it would cheer me on my way greatly. Poor human nature sometimes craves human aid; now, my family and friends all gone to the other and better land, I seek for sympathy from the friends of Jesus."

Without a legal claim upon Methodism the daughter of a man who gave forty-four years to the Church— the fruits of whose labors, with that of his heroic associates, appear in great Conferences numbering many thousand church members—had a moral claim that could not be ignored without grave wrong.

The author investigated the case and found it to be as we have already described. He authorized her transfer from the poor-house to a comfortable home ; he interested others in the story, and secured contributions to provide for her until the Conference which her father helped found came to her relief. The day this veteran's daughter went "over the hill from the poor-house" she wrote these words as the conclusion of a tender, tearful, thankful letter: "O, how good the Lord has been, and how he has helped me all these dark years. It has been a thorny way, but Christ has led me, blessed be his name, and the crown is now but just a little way ahead; 'tis mine, 'tis mine, I know it. Jesus says it; 'tis true. And now, dear brother, let me thank you again and again, and I know heaven will bless you. Yours in Christ."

* * * * * *

The next story from real life is taken from recent numbers of the California *Christian Advocate.* Nos. I and II are editorials, No. III is a contribution.

I.

"Rev. Stanford Ing is not dead, but only superannuated, which is far worse. He belongs to the St. Louis Conference, and has been a pioneer, a vidette on the picket-line, all the time. He is a hero and almost a martyr for Christ's sake. The Church has used him as a bearer of great burdens, a toiler in one of its hardest vineyards. He has lived and wrought uncomplainingly and most devotedly, for he has been a saint as well as a hero. Stanford Ing has stood wintry storms and summer heat, and fought with

5

' wild beasts,' as Paul called them, a hundred times. He had a tough, wiry constitution, and so lived on amid great perils and labors until old age compelled him to stop. At the last session of the St. Louis Conference this veteran minister asked for a superannuated relation. Scarred and worn and old and weather-beaten, he had to cease going out to the battle. His brethren were deeply affected. They wept, they shouted, they gathered around their aged friend and brother, and embraced him and shook his withered hand. Now we hope that Brother Ing has enough to keep him from the poor-house the rest of his life. A sort of faint remembrance runs through our mind that he has a farm or a house and lot, or something of the kind. At all events, he is now superannuated. He may have saved his old clothes and laid up some old shoes, and his aged and frugal wife may have gathered up a few things. If they have not done this, God pity them! We had the curiosity to look up the record as found in Rev. Jay Benson Hamilton's little paper, *Our Veterans*, and see just what Rev. Stanford Ing is likely to get from his Conference, now he is old and broken down and superannuated. He will receive just about $62 a year,* and

---

* These figures are taken from a table giving average allowances by Annual Conferences.

if he should die his widow would get $13 a year—
that is, the Methodist Episcopal Church takes the
man's last inch of strength and life and then turns
him out to die on the munificent endowment of $62
a year.   Nobody helps any but the St. Louis Conference, and that, after doing its best, has only $62 for
Brother Ing.   Indeed, the brethren do well to weep
at Brother Ing's superannuation.   We can scarcely
refrain from weeping every time we see an aged minister superannuated, unless we know he has enough
to live on.   The very largest sum given to any superannuated man is $300 ; the annual gifts run from
that down to $5.   Yes, some superannuated men get
$5, some $7, some $20, and so on up to $300, and
then beneficence utterly breaks down.   Here, then, is
a spectacle.   Stanford Ing is as much our brother as
if he belonged to California.   He spends a long life
in heroic work, and the Church even cannot force
him into another battle-field, but dismisses him with
the magnificent sum of $62 a year.   If you would
like to know what we privately think of that, call, and
we will tell you what we do not wish to publish.   No
wonder aged ministers pray that they 'may cease at
once to work and live.'   The very best done for any
of our veteran, broken-down ministers is pitifully in-
adequate.   The worst done is criminal, and makes one

mad. Stanford Ing ought to be supported handsome-
ly and without a single burden to the end. He de-
serves a palace and a throne, and God will give him
these. 'O Lord, how long?'"

II.

"Rev. Stanford Ing was superannuated at the last
session of his Conference. He is a fair specimen of
a type of itinerant preachers that may die out, though
we hope not. He was a pioneer, brave, true, and
useful. Our editorial produced unexpected results.
It was noticed beyond any hope we had of it. Some
time after it was published a lady called at our house
and said : 'I have read your article on Stanford Ing,
and I think such men ought not to suffer. Please
send this to him,' and she handed us $100. We sent
that to Brother Ing, and have before us his receipt
for it and a touching letter. He says: 'Your letter
came duly to hand, bringing to me a draft for $100,
for which I do most sincerely thank the unknown
donor, and you I do most heartily thank for such
kind attention. I do not understand it ; it has wholly
taken me by surprise.   I said on the Conference floor at the time of my superannuation, "The
inevitable has come and I cheerfully submit, but it
has come at a time that I am less prepared for it than

I have been for twenty years." My Conference gave me $75. But to think that this gift of $100 has come to me from the Pacific coast so unexpectedly overcomes me. You said it came from God. Very well, as such I receive it and thank him. But his instrument comes nearer to my senses, and I can understand it better. So I do most sincerely thank you and the unknown lady, and I ask you to convey to her the thanks of myself and wife. We shall ever remember her. The gift comes to us opportunely, as it will help us to prepare a home and shelter for the coming winter. We will make it serve the best ends possible.' The rest of his letter is entirely private.

"This affair discloses one of those sorrowful depths we dread to look into. Surely, the Methodist Episcopal Church will not permit the shameless and wicked impoverishment of worn-out and aged ministers to continue. We have determined to begin somewhere, law or no law, and help some of these suffering men in their old age. The cases should be taken up *seriatim*, if no other way, and helped. We have but little patience with vain excuses about the matter. We, too, thank the Christian lady who sent the $100 to a poor, aged, and broken-down preacher. The California Conference is able to take care of its own dependent preachers and their widows. We suggest for this year a Veterans' Day; for instance, the first Sunday in August, and a careful effort to do a most blessed deed of love and charity. We do not dwell upon this case for any purpose but to glorify God and help worthy men."

III.

" Having read with considerable interest the articles in the *California Advocate* concerning Rev. Stanford Ing, a recent superannuate of the St. Louis Conference, I have thought it only due to that grand old man, and likely to help the cause of the superannuates, to give some reminiscences of his life when Missouri's brave sons were called to stand :

' Between their loved home and the war's desolation.'

" In the summer of 1861 the Thirteenth Regiment of Illinois Volunteer Infantry, Colonel John B. Wyman commanding, was guarding the town of Rolla, Mo., the then terminus of the S. W. P. R. R., and the depot of supplies for the Army of the South-west. One morning a tall, thin man about fifty years of age, dressed in black, approached the guard-line and asked to be conveyed to head-quarters. When in the presence of the commanding officer, he stated that he was a Methodist minister in charge of a circuit occu-pying the surrounding country. He also stated that his people and himself were Union in sentiment, and because of this had been subject to continuous annoy-ance from secession neighbors and armed guerrillas. His male members, he further stated, were then hid-ing in the woods and caves, being driven from their homes by armed bands, and if the women and chil-dren could be brought into Rolla and protected, the men were ready to enlist in the United States service. Satisfying himself that the statements of the stranger were true, the colonel fitted out one or two companies of mounted infantry to go out and bring in the women and children.   When about to start the stranger turned to the colonel and said :

" ' Colonel, you have armed all these men, but you have given me no weapons.'

" ' O,' said the colonel, ' you're a preacher, and are not expected to fight.'

" ' Sir,' said the stranger, gravely, ' I have not preached a sermon for the last six months but my stewards and class-leaders have had to stand on either side of the pulpit armed ready to protect me while I preached.   I think it is time to fight as well as pray, and if you will furnish the tools I will show you whether I can use them or not.'

"The colonel, pleased with his spirit, furnished this man, Rev. Stanford Ing, with a complete cavalry outfit, and in the first encounter with the guerrillas the reverend gentleman brought in three or four of the enemy as prisoners of war. His daring and true military spirit charmed the officers in charge of the expedition, and on the return of Brother Ing and his male members they were mustered into the United States service as cavalry, and their pastor commissioned as captain. The class-leaders and stewards became commissioned and non-commissioned officers, and a veritable Methodist church was suddenly transformed into a military company.

"The captain held his class-meetings, prayer-meetings, and preaching services as regularly as circumstances would allow. I was a frequent attendant at the captain's religious services, and received much encouragement from him in my purpose to enter the ministry if I should live to get out of the war.

"This militant church became the body-guard of General Curtis, and at the battle of Pea Ridge did such gallant service that the general, in taking leave of them shortly after, said:

"'I have never had under my command braver or more faithful soldiers than these praying and fighting Methodists.'

" While a brave officer and a thorough Union man, hating secession as treason, Rev. Stanford Ing never allowed himself to forget the Christian courtesy due to even an enemy.   At Batesville, Ark., was a nice brick church belonging to the Methodist Episcopal Church, South.   Coming to my tent one day, he said :

" ' I have been to the general and have obtained per-mission to use the Methodist church for preaching services, so as to prevent its being taken for hospital uses, in which event the property would be greatly damaged.   Now, come with me and we will call on the preacher, tell him what we have done, and get the key.'

" We went.   The preacher was a young man and a pronounced secessionist.   He treated our proposition with profound contempt, and said some very insulting things.   The captain was aroused, and ordered the young man to at once accompany us to the sexton and get the key.   We occupied the church as we con-templated, but the irate pastor never appeared at any of our meetings, though frequently invited.   When our command left the town we turned over the key to the pastor, and the church was in as good condi-tion as when we first entered it.

" After our departure other troops came in, and the

church was seized and used as a hospital, and greatly injured.

"Captain Ing was greatly beloved, not only by his own men, but by all the troops who came in contact with him. It is sad to think that so heroic a man should be turned out in his old age to browse upon the cold, bleak moors of this world's charity with the single alleviation of $75 a year from the Conference.

"The heroic spirit of our old men in the ministry, whose salaries in their prime were scarcely adequate for their then present wants, challenges our admiration and cries loudly for better support in their decrepitude.

"The captain's military career was by no means his most heroic labor, though no braver man ever drew the sword or more gallantly led a cavalry charge than he, but it was that self-sacrificing labor he bestowed upon his circuits before and after the war, where low salaries and hard work were the uniform experience that was most heroic of all. Many of our old men have stood as gallantly by our country in its emergencies, and have toiled as patiently as he, and therefore deserve, as does our hero, the most generous and kindly support."

*   *   *   *   *   *

If any deem these exaggerations and exceptional in character, we have but a single word of reply. We have but begun; but we have gathered a large number of incidents which are authentic as the records of actual personal experience. They are as pitiful and pathetic as ever romancer imagined. At an early date we shall give them to the Church. They will be sad and sorrowful; some of them will be terrible and tragic. It is not shameful to reveal these facts; it is sinful to permit them to exist. The evil can only be remedied by being made known. To all criticisms or denunciations we have no reply to offer but the epigram of a reformer whom the whole nation delighted to honor when dead. The men who mobbed him became the fathers of children who built a monument to him. His words are a motto well worthy every great reform:

"I am aware that many object to the severity of my language; but is there not cause for severity? I will be as harsh as truth, as uncompromising as justice. On this subject I do not wish to think, speak, or write with moderation. I am in earnest—I will not equivocate, I will not excuse, I will not retreat a single inch, and I WILL BE HEARD. The apathy of the people is enough to make every statue leap from its pedestal and to hasten the resurrection of the dead."—WILLIAM LLOYD GARRISON.

DISSOLVING VIEWS OF THE METHODISM OF 1989

I RECEIVED a letter from the widow of a Methodist preacher which inclosed a manuscript, found among her husband's papers after his death, addressed to me. It was an incident intended to help create an interest in a great reform dear to his heart :

" YOUR OLD MEN SHALL DREAM DREAMS." Joel ii, 28.

My wife met me at the door of the parsonage yesterday as I returned from an afternoon's pastoral visiting. She was greatly agitated and bitterly weeping. Alarmed and astonished, I said : " What is it, my dear ? "

With difficulty she regained her composure enough to speak. After a moment's sobbing, she said :

" Rev. William Brown, a superannuated minister, is in the parlor, and I want you to ask him to spend Thanksgiving with us."

" Is that what you are crying about ? " I said, as I

playfully patted her wet cheeks. For a moment her lips trembled, as if she must weep again, and then her face brightened into a smile.

"Perhaps I am foolish," she said, "but he called at the door to sell pins, needles, and notions. He said he was an old preacher compelled by necessity to try to earn his bread. He was so badly crippled with rheumatism that he could hardly walk. He seemed so frail and feeble that I invited him in to rest a little while. I told him you would be glad to see him. When I thought that we might, like him, come to want and distress in our old age it almost broke my heart. I just had to cry."

Old Brother Brown was very glad to see me. He apologized for accepting my wife's kind invitation, but frankly said :

"I could not have gone much farther without resting. I am getting to be quite old and feeble now, you see. My widowed daughter, who has a houseful of little folks to care for, gives me a place in her little home, and I must try and help her earn our bread."

I easily secured his consent to remain over night, and join us in our Thanksgiving dinner on the morrow. He was seventy-two years of age. He had preached for fifty years, and had received an average salary of $260 a year. His allowance as a superannuate was

$50 a year. He was very reserved about himself. He skillfully evaded all references to his own need or manner of living. He was shabbily and scantily dressed. He was to all appearances thin and ill from lack of proper nourishment. He was happy and cheerful; he never made a single complaint. He constantly referred with thankfulness to the many mercies God had bestowed on him. He bubbled over with reminiscences of his early ministry. The privations and hardships of his itinerancy while young and vigorous were described with all the zest and pride with which a valiant soldier relates his battles and victories. At the supper-table I found my wife making great effort to conceal her emotion. I caught the contagion, and had once to wipe away a stray tear with my napkin. Old Brother Brown was very hungry, but his natural politeness had a severe tax to restrain within the bounds of propriety his vigorous appetite. Wife, with the skill and tact of a shrewd woman, continually tempted our guest to further eating after each movement which he made as if he was going to stop. She had some little delicacy or tidbit she herself had prepared, and wanted his opinion upon its quality. When he expressed a favorable opinion, as he did every time, she insisted upon his trying a little more. Between the demands of his great hunger and my wife's little deceptions our aged brother ate until he had enough.

After supper we were sitting in the parlor and he was resting quietly in the easy-chair, when he dropped off into a gentle doze. After a few moments of quiet he burst out into a hearty laugh, and said, gleefully : " Why, Francis Asbury! Are you back again ? What do you want this time ? "

Awakened by his own laugh, he arose and walked to and fro for a little while, as if in deep thought. He then sat down again in the easy-chair, and said to me :

" Do you believe in dreams ? "

I replied I did, if they were good dreams ; I always doubted bad ones. He laughed heartily, as if remembering his own dream.

" One of the old prophets said : ' Your old men shall dream dreams.' I always ridiculed dreams, and thought it very strange that Joel should associate dreaming with the outpouring of the Spirit. But I had a dream last Thanksgiving eve. If you would like to hear it I will relate it. Perhaps you would better write it down. It may amuse your little ones when they get older.

" The day before Thanksgiving last year I was greatly worried. Our rent was over-due. Our landlord had been very pressing in his demands. He finally threatened that if the rent was not paid very soon, we would be turned into the street. My daughter's illness had prevented her earning as much as usual. My rheumatism had shut me in a great deal, and we were very sorely pressed. I had found myself growing bitter and censorious toward the Church. I often complained to my daughter that the Church I had served so long and so faithfully had forgotten me. I had not decent clothing to wear, and had to stay at home from church. Our rent was unpaid and our larder was empty, and to-morrow was Thanksgiving. Poor thing, she was white and thin, as much from lack of food as from sickness, but her smile was sweet and her words bright and cheerful as she said:

"'O, no! father; the Church does not forget us. And I am very sure the Lord will not; for he said: "I will never leave thee nor forsake thee." I cannot always see, father, dear; but I trust him all the time. We will have a happy Thanksgiving to-morrow, even if it is a fast-day with us all. I am sorry for the children'—and her voice trembled a little—'I am sorry for you, my dear old father. I am so glad I have for a father a veteran who has been a hero in so many conflicts. I don't believe after fifty years of valiant service he is going to become a coward and lower his colors now.'

" I kissed her white face, and said :

" ' God bless you, my child.   Your old father fears he is too heavy a burden for these weak shoulders to bear much longer.   I am in a hurry to get home for your sake.'

" She simply smiled, and said :

" ' It will be time to seek better quarters or worse when I turn you out.'

" While she was out trying to earn a little money for our Thanksgiving day's bread, her youngest child, a little fellow, came to me and said, in a sturdy boy-fashion :

" ' Grandpa, I don't believe the Bible is true.'

" I smiled at his earnestness, and said :

" ' Well, go and bring it in and we w ll burn it up. We don't want any lying book about this house.'

" He hurried into his mother's bedroom and brought me the old family Bible.   He held it and looked at it a little while without speaking, and then said :

" ' I hate to burn it, grandpa.   Mother will miss it so much.   You will miss it, too.   Us children will miss its beautiful stories.   It's grandma's book, too ; she used to read it to us before she died.   I guess we won't burn it just yet, if it does tell one lie.'

6

" ' Where does it tell a lie, my son ? '

" He quickly turned to Psalm xxxvii, 25, and read : ' I have been young and now am old ; yet have I not seen the righteous forsaken, nor his seed begging bread.'

" No infidel ever so completely puzzled me in all my ministry as did that little fellow, with piercing eye and ringing voice, as he said :

" ' There ! what did I tell you ! '

" I knew that many nights this little brood had gone to bed hungry. I knew that there was not a mouthful in the house and no prospect for a bite for the Thanksgiving dinner to-morrow, save begging. I tried to speak, but could not, and, bursting into tears, I hurried to my own room and tried to pray. I could not pray. All the hard, bitter things I had thought, but had refused to cherish, now poured in upon me. I began to turn them over in my mind as a sweet morsel, and really took great comfort in feeling so miserable. My mood was made more bitter by hearing the sigh of my daughter as she entered the house, which told me her effort was fruitless. Our Thanksgiving was destined to be a day of fasting. I determined to write an article for *The Christian Advocate* in which I would free my mind and tell some wholesome, bitter truths. It took me a long while, as

I write very slowly now. After I had finished it I
was surprised to find it so short. I smiled to find it
as biting as it was brief. I said, with a grim smile :

" ' It does not take much caustic to create a blister;
this, I guess, will make several.'

" I began with a contrast between modern and
olden-time Methodism. I pictured the worldliness of
the Church ; the selfishness of the ministers ; the am-
bition of the officials ; and ended by predicting that
the class-meeting would be given up ; the prayer-meet-
.ing would freeze up, and the sources of spiritual
activity would dry up ; the pulpit would become a
platform ; the church would become a club ; public
worship would degenerate into a popular gathering
in which oratory and operatic singing would combine
to make a service which it would be blasphemy to call
religious or sacred.

" As I read it aloud I forgot my hunger and pain,
and laughed aloud as I said :

" ' That will make them smart and writhe.'

" I heard a gentle rap at the door, and, thinking it
was my daughter, I said :

" ' Come in.'

" The door opened and a man entered. He was old
and dressed in the costume of the ministers of my
boyhood days. A shad-bellied coat, surmounted with

a white choker, knee-breeches, long stockings, and low shoes made him seem like a picture of the olden times.

" He made a profound bow, and said :

" ' Is this Dr. Brown ? '

" I said :

" ' My name is Brown, but I am no doctor.'

" ' Indeed !' said he. ' I came to see you because I was informed you were about to doctor Methodism.'

" ' Who are you ? ' I said, a little impatiently.

" ' I am an angel,' he gravely replied.

" I suspected he was crazy, and said, a little curtly :

" ' You may be an angel, but if you are you are the first I ever saw in a shad-bellied coat and knee-breeches. Where are your wings ? '

" ' I don't need any wings. I have a flying-machine outside. I want you to take a ride with me.'

" I knew now he was crazy, and decided it would be wise to humor him. I said :

" ' I am a little afraid of those new-fangled ma-chines. I prefer one I can handle easily. When I go out for a long midnight trip I always ride a broom. But what is your name ? '

" ' Francis Asbury,' was the answer, a little sternly, as if he resented my last remark.

" I looked at him closely and recognized him at once. I turned from him to look at the large steel engraving which hung upon the wall.   I noticed the striking likeness, and said :

"'I am glad to see you, Bishop Asbury.   You have not changed much, save for the better.   You seem younger than when you died.'

"Without answering me, the bishop took up my article for *The Christian Advocate,* and, glancing at the heading, read aloud :

"'Forsake not the old paths.'

"'That is good,' said he, and proceeded to read it aloud.

"It seemed so unkind, so unfair, and so unchristian that I was heartily ashamed.   After reading it, my strange guest looked at me intently for an instant, and then, as his face lighted up with a smile of great beauty, he said, cheerily :

"'Old comrade, it can't be that bad.'

"To be called comrade by a bishop greatly startled me, until I remembered that he had been dead for a hundred years.

"Asbury went on :

"'I have had my eye upon you of late.   I have watched you growing bitter and harsh.   Your privations are souring your spirit.   You are beginning to censure and slander the Church you have served for fifty years.   You cannot afford to spoil the record of half a century by a few uncharitable words in your old age. Your comrades are sweet, cheerful, and patient. They rarely ever murmur or complain. Will you be the first to dishonor the veteran legion by becoming an old scold? If you are determined to disgrace yourself and us we will save our credit and your honor by asking our Commander to discharge you from the service. I want to show you the Methodism of 1989. You will be the first to laugh at the foolish caricature contained in your predictions in this article. You will be sorry you ever wrote it.'

" While he was speaking he led me out of the house, and assisted me to a seat in a strange-looking vehicle. It seemed to rise and move off like a bird. Asbury said :

" 'We are in 1989. This is a flying-machine. You remember you ridiculed the possibility of flying, once.'

" I recalled the very sermon in which I denounced the hair-brained folly of tempting God by attempting to fly.

" ' It isn't safe to prophesy,' said Asbury. 'It may be you are as much mistaken about Methodism as you were about the flying-machine.'

" I was too humbled to reply.

" After a few moments Asbury said :

" ' Here is a Methodist class-meeting; let us go in and see what it is like.'

"The room was neat, attractive, and cozy. It was filled by a happy, hearty company, whose faces indicated that they had religion and enjoyed it. The service began with a hymn. I recognized it, and my heart leaped within me as every voice joined in singing. The leader, an old man, said:

" ' Precious hymn of olden time! When I was a little child my grandmother used to sing that very hymn. She said her father, a heroic veteran of the cross, used to take her on his knee and sing it. His name was Rev. William Brown. He was very poor all his life. He had a very hard time, but he never complained. He led many souls to Christ and counted all his trials and sorrows but light afflictions which only made his crown of glory brighter and more beautiful.'

"I felt so ashamed I could scarcely refrain from bursting into tears. How I despised that miserable old *Advocate* article, and wondered what had ever become of it. When I remembered how capacious Dr. Buckley's waste-basket was I cherished a hope that perhaps it had found in it a dishonorable burial, never to find a resurrection.

"You can hardly imagine my feelings as I sat in

that class-meeting, led by my daughter's grandson, a hundred years after I was dead. The meeting was cheerful, instructive, and spiritual. Near the close of the meeting a young man arose, and said :

" ' I have been greatly interested in an old book which our leader loaned me this week. It was a little memorial volume of his grandmother's father, Rev. William Brown. It described his privations and sufferings. The record of his faithful labors was very impressive. He toiled for half a century with hardly enough to eat or wear. His family were often without food ; yet he never was known to complain. He was sweet and cheerful and hopeful. He was accustomed to say to his children and grandchildren : " To preach the Gospel of Christ is the highest honor ever bestowed upon a human being. It is such a privilege and blessing to win souls to my Master that I wonder I have been counted worthy to share in this holy work. In it bread and water are a royal feast. My labors have been so worthless, and my wages so great, that I have been infinitely over-paid, and now in addition I am to have eternal life."

" ' Brothers and sisters, I have long wavered as to my own duty But as I have read this brief story of the sainted hero who has been in heaven for a hundred years, I covet his joy and want to win a crown

like his. God has called me to preach, and I obey
him. From this time forward I shall devote myself
to my Master's service.'

"I broke down and sobbed aloud. They did not
notice it, as immediately a regular old-fashioned
shouting melody burst forth from every heart and
mouth. Asbury hurried me out, and we flew on.

"'Here is a church with a public service about to
begin; let us join in the worship,' said Asbury.

"The room was large and plain. It was crowded.
The moment I entered I exclaimed:

"'Here is what I have been long wanting to see.
A perfectly ventilated church. The air is as pure as
it is out-doors.'

"'That is so,' said Asbury; 'I wonder how they
do it.'

"The service was simple, earnest, and hearty. The
preacher was a man in the prime of life, vivacious,
practical, and full of common sense. One striking
feature was the music. A powerful pipe-organ, a
grand piano, and a full orchestra supported and accompanied the solo and chorus singing of a large and
well-trained choir. The people all sang sweetly and
soulfully.

" Asbury said :

"'Methodism has robbed the theater and ball-room

of their chief charm. Music is one of her most powerful agencies. The best music in every community
now is heard in the Methodist Church.'

"By some mysterious arrangement the house could
be darkened instantaneously, and a stereopticon picture of great beauty was thrown upon the wall at the
right of the preacher. It had a charming and impressive effect.

"Asbury said:

"'Methodism has borrowed from Roman Catholi-
cism pictorial illustrations of religious truth. Art
and music are now, as in the earlier Church, the hand-
maids of religion. The best artists confine themselves, as did the old masters, almost wholly to religious and biblical subjects.'

"The sermon was from the text, 'Forsake not the
old paths.' I cringed as it was announced, as I remembered that slanderous article I had written about
Methodism. The pastor said in his introduction that
the sermon had grown out of a simple incident, almost
an accident.

"'I received from an aged relative an old book. It
was a memorial of my father's grandfather, Rev.
William Brown. He was one of the pioneer itinerants, who helped lay the foundations of Methodism.
He had served the Church fifty years for a bare pit-

tance, but he had greatly blessed the Church by his labors.   Many strong churches grew out of the feeble societies he planted.   The conversions during his ministry were several thousand, among whom were scores of ministers.   The little book contained the funeral addresses, the obituary, published in *The Christian Advocate*, and testimonials to his fidelity and patience, to his unruffled sweetness of disposition, and spotless purity of life.   He was the instrument, under God, of the beginning of this church.   He preached in the old school-house when this great city was a small village.   He helped build the first church and preached one year as its pastor.   I have a great surprise, and I know a great pleasure, in store for you.'   Instantly the house was darkened and my portrait was shown in a beautiful stereopticon picture.

"Bishop Asbury said :

"' You have not changed much, save for the better ; you look younger than you did when you died.'

"I found my heart full almost to bursting as the preacher, with fiery eloquence, urged the congregation to emulate the faithfulness and imitate the spiritual activity of the very days I had denounced in my scandalous libel as worldly, selfish, and corrupt.   I tried to rise and confess my unworthiness to receive all this eulogy, but Asbury hurried me out, and we flew on.

" ' We are now going to attend a Methodist Annual Conference,' he said.

" It was in a large city. The church was a magnificent temple upon the principal street. We were in time for the opening exercises. The Conference began just as it did the first session I attended when a boy, seeking admission on trial.

> " ' And are we yet alive
> And see each other's face ?
> Glory and praise to Jesus give
> For his redeeming grace.'

" The old hymn made the arches of the great temple echo and re-echo as the preachers sang with lusty fervor.

" The ritual service for the sacrament, unchanged in a single word, seemed like an echo of other days which subdued and melted my soul. The printed list of preachers and their hosts was read with delight.

" ' I was afraid they would have a Conference Bureau of Entertainment and would board the preachers out,' I said.

" Asbury replied :

" ' No; Methodist hospitality, like Methodist theology, never grows old.'

" The routine of Conference business was but little

changed. The addresses at the anniversaries sounded very familiar. I even recognized some things in the episcopal address to the candidates for admission and for ordination. The session at which the characters of the elders were called for examination was a great surprise to me. I expected each man to arise and state the contributions of his church toward the benevolences, mentioning all by name, and whether or not he had reached the ten million dollar line, and add as a postscript how many subscribers he had secured for *The Christian Advocate* and the *Methodist Review.* Imagine my surprise when each man answering to his name spoke of his own religious experience and the spiritual condition of the work which had been committed to him. The report was not about dollars, but souls. Interruptions by song and shout were frequent. It seemed like a gigantic old-fashioned class-meeting. I myself shouted several times. I think Asbury did once or twice, too. When it was over the bishop led the Conference in a tender prayer for the baptism of the Holy Spirit.

"I asked Asbury:

"'When do they report their collections?'

"'That is all changed. The Church does not exalt standards; she inculcates principles. Methodist giving has long since passed the Jewish standard of one tenth.   Our people give to all benevolences without any " brass band " appeals.   Our ministers do their duty without any Conference advertisement of either success or failure.   The Church recognizes that ministers are not ordained to raise collections or secure subscribers to Church periodicals, but to preach the Gospel and save souls.'

" I noticed that old men were treated with a deference almost like reverence.

" Asbury, noticing my surprise, said :

" ' The Church has learned that experience is as valuable to the minister as to the physician or lawyer. Old men are valued in the ministry as in all other professions.   Age is no barrier to the best places. The white head is a crown of honor.   The young man does not step from the theological seminary to the great metropolitan pulpit.   He is placed upon probation, after the good old fashion.   The hard work is all done by the young men.   If there is an easy place or light work it is always reserved for the feeble old man.   Ordination to the ministry receives its full recognition now.   Every living minister of pure life and character is given such work as he is able to do.   The old and broken-down veteran is the beloved ward of the Church, and all his wants are lovingly and bountifully supplied, not as a charity, but as a just and honest debt.'

"The Veterans' Anniversary was the great event of the Conference session. A member of the Conference who was to superannuate preached his semi-centennial sermon. It was no mournful lament, but a ringing, rousing battle-cry. It was full of reminiscences and sparkled with fun. The old hero looked back over fifty years of service with joyful pride; he looked forward to an evening time of rest with composure and peace. Among many incidents which illustrated his address one made a very strong impression upon me. It compared 1989 with 1889, greatly to the latter's discredit.

"The speaker said:

"'I have had a glimpse of one feature of our Church history which modern historians take no delight in recording. The neglect of the veterans in the first century of Methodism was cruel and shameful. It was not an intentional wrong, but one of the accidents of the marvelous expansion and growth of the Church. In a hurried march or a forced retreat soldiers are more anxious to conquer or escape than to care or provide for those who fall out by the way.

"'I have a friend who is somewhat of an antiquarian. He has had re-printed as a curiosity a fragment of a sensational romance entitled *From the Pulpit to the Poor-house.* It was published about a century ago. The name of the author is unknown. A fragment of the title-page gave it as " Rev. Jay Bens—." This is supposed to be a portion of the *nom de plume* of an anonymous writer. The author portrayed the sufferings of an itinerant who was neglected until he was about to be taken by the town authorities as a pauper to a charitable institution. The story breaks off abruptly just as the old minister and his wife are placed in a carriage to take the train for the poor-house. The concluding chapters are lost.

" ' While the romance is confessedly of the character of works like *Uncle Tom's Cabin,* we find from letters from veterans included in the romance, as well as from the history of the Church, that much of the stir it created was because it was too true to life to make comfortable reading for either the laity or ministry. My antiquarian friend has printed with it an engraving of a famous picture hanging in the historical gallery of the Methodist Museum in the city of Manhattan. An excursion to this the greatest city in the world will be the event of one's life, if time is taken to visit the Methodist Book Emporium. No such building is on the globe to-day. The immense wing set apart as a museum for the rare products of

Methodist archæology is one of the wonders of our time. In the great picture gallery, among a vast collection of portraits and historical scenes is one of mournful, almost tragic, interest. It is entitled "The Lost Brother Found." It is a Conference scene. Bishop Gilbert Haven is introducing to a Methodist Conference one of the members, who had been found in the alms-house. The bishop had clothed the aged brother in a new suit and was presenting him to the Conference, who were standing upon their feet, being led in the doxology by Chaplain McCabe. The portraits of the bishop and the chaplain are masterpieces. But with infinite art the veteran is placed so as to conceal his face. The long gray hair, the attitude, and pose of the old man are so pathetic that one cannot behold it without tears. This picture is engraved as a frontispiece for the fragment of the tale *From the Pulpit to the Poor-house*. As I carefully examined the picture and read and re-read the story, my heart was filled with gratitude to God that all this shame and suffering is over.

"'The veterans now are the honored and beloved wards of the Church. We are never without occupation while able to work. When unable for further labor our glorious Church smoothes our way to the grave with loving and generous bounty.'

7

"One incident during the Conference session was the culmination of all the humiliating experiences of this wonderful night.

"The Conference suspended its business to give place to a special anniversary service. This session of the Annual Conference was the one hundred and fiftieth anniversary of the founding of the church which was entertaining it. Addresses of remarkable interest recorded the wonderful history of the century and a half just closing. The last address was by a layman whose princely contributions to all benevolences had made this great church the standard-bearer of the denomination for many years. His address was simple, pathetic, and powerful. It was a graphic description of the founding of the church in weakness and poverty. The struggle of the little handful of people, the heroic devotion and faithfulness of the young preacher who was the first pastor of the church, were portrayed in words that thrilled the vast audience to tears and cheers alternately   The speaker said:

"'I desire, in closing, to relate a simple incident and give you a delightful surprise:

"'My father was the grandson of a Methodist preacher. The old minister lived with his widowed daughter, his only surviving child. They were desperately poor and often were without food. One evening before Thanksgiving there was nothing to eat in the house.   My father, who was then a small lad, said to his grandfather :

" ' " Grandpa, I don't believe the Bible is true."

" ' " Well, go and bring it to me, and we will burn it. We don't want any lying book about this house."

" ' My father brought the book, but said :

" ' " I hate to burn it, grandpa, mother will miss it so much. You will miss it, and we will all miss it. It was grandma's book, and I hate to burn any thing she loved. I guess we will keep it, if it does tell one lie."

" ' " Where does it tell a lie, my son ? "

" ' My father read to him Psalm xxxvii, 25 : " I have been young, and now am old ; yet have I not seen the righteous forsaken, nor his seed begging bread," and said :

" ' " There ! what did I tell you ! "

" ' His grandfather burst into tears and hurried away to pray My father cried himself to sleep that night because he had made his old grandfather weep. The only time the subject ever was mentioned afterward, the old minister said, in a trembling voice :

" ' " My son, this book is God's word. He is our best Friend. He loves all his children ; he loves you. Give him your heart, and you will understand his word ; or, what is better, you will trust and love him even when you do not understand him."

" 'My father early gave God his heart. God blessed him with a large family, of whom I am the youngest. All became Christians. If I have ever done any thing to bless the world and help the Church I owe it to my father. He gave me, as his most valued treas-ure, the very old Bible he wanted once to burn. Here it is. Precious book ! I would not sell it for a thou-sand dollars. It is holy from the touch of that hon-ored veteran, who, in his early ministry, founded this church and was its first pastor. I have had painted an oil portrait of our first pastor, my father's heroic grandfather, Rev. William Brown, to be hung in our beautiful chapel.'

" The portrait was unveiled and presented to the bishop, who responded in a tender and thrilling speech. He closed by saying that he was all the more gratified to have a share in this historic service, as the man whose memory we thus honor was his mother's grandfather.

"Asbury led me out convulsed with emotion. I said to Asbury :

" 'O, that miserable article ! I can never be really happy in heaven until I find Dr. Buckley, and know for certain that he buried it in his waste-basket and sent it to the paper-mill to be ground into pulp. What if, after all, it should yet be discovered to vex and shame my honored posterity.'

"Asbury smiled, and said:

"'Don't worry, old comrade, I have that article in my pocket. Nobody ever saw it but you and me.'

"I was so delighted that I turned to embrace the bishop, and I woke up.

"Before me, upon the table where I had left the article, 'Forsake not the old Paths,' I found a basket filled with every thing needed for a princely Thanksgiving dinner—turkey, vegetables, and all. Nuts and candy for the children showed that even the little ones were not forgotten. A card was in the basket, which said:

"'When next we ride together, you will never return.   FRANCIS ASBURY.'

"I have never once in the year now ending had the slightest desire to complain of the Lord or his Church. Our life is full of privation, but it is full of trust, joy, and peace. I have never met Asbury since until to-night while I was dozing. I thought I saw him and heard him say:

"'We will have another ride together to-night, old comrade.'

" Perhaps I will have another dream to-night.   If
I do I will tell you all about it in the morning."

In the morning we knocked to arouse our guest for
breakfast, but he made no reply.   We opened the
door and found that Brother Brown had gone off with
Bishop Asbury to receive his crown.   He left his old
worn and crippled body behind, which we laid away
tenderly in the village church-yard until he should
want it again.

TOM THE PHARISEE AND JACK THE PRODIGAL.

CHAPTER I.

JACK THE PRODIGAL.

"HELLO, Prod., you have returned to your father's house, I see, and I am commanded to kill the fatted calf; only the calf is a hen. How do you like traveling on foot to the far country?"

"Look here, Pharrie, old chap, don't tease so; go easy on my travels. I can say harder things about my making such a fool of myself than you will dare to do. When I read the prodigal story I used to say the boy that ran away was a fool, but the boy that stayed at home was a knave. I'd just as soon be a prodigal as a Pharisee. You see, when we were put up you had all the piety intended for both of us and I had to take the deviltry of both to even it up. I am glad to get home, and you can't drive me away again, if you tease and torment me every hour of the day as you only can."

"Forgive me, Jack, I was only fooling. Nobody is gladder to see you home again than I am. Only I do want to know all about your adventures; how you escaped us, and how you were captured. Come, now, own up, and tell me the whole business, and I will promise never to tease you again, at least about that scrape."

"Don't make that promise, Tom, for I know you can't keep it, and you have enough sins to answer for now. But I am perfectly willing to tell you all about my running away. It took me longer to do it than it will to tell about it. When that plaguey old yellow fife which I played in the fife and drum corps whispered to me, 'Go to war; you will find it easy to climb from the drum corps to be drum-major, and then it will be but a step from drum-major to major-general,' like a great stupid I believed it all and started on foot with my every-day clothes on, not a cent of money, and no baggage but my old fife. I laid out the first night at the railroad station, intending to slip off the next morning with the enlisted men who were camping out while waiting for the special train. A good-hearted soldier shared his blanket with me, and I fared pretty well, although I was tired and hungry. About daylight the train arrived and I tried to slip aboard. I had just taken a seat at one end of the

car when you and father came in at the other end.
I dodged out like a flash and made a flying leap into
a clump of bushes and hid until the train had gone.
When I thought it safe to start I found my yellow
fife with which I was to blow my way to fame was
lost. It broke me all up, but I determined I would
not back out, and I took up my march toward the
camp one hundred miles away. I traveled all day,
too proud to beg and afraid to steal. At a large
town, which I reached about nine o'clock at night, I
found a train about to move out, and I got aboard.
When the conductor appeared I tried to make some
excuse about having no money. He very curtly said
to the brakeman, 'Help this passenger to get off at
the next station.' When it was time to get off I was
in no hurry, but the brakeman was, and as he helped
me down he held my collar for fear I might fall. It
was dark as pitch, pouring rain, and the mud was six
inches deep. A drunken man who had to be helped
off just the same as me said :

"'Where you goin'—hic—Bub ? '

"I told him I did not know.

"'Run away from home—hic—haint you, Bub ?—
hic.'

"I would have cried if I had been alone when he
said 'home.' I could see every one of you, and you

were all at table eating one of mother's good suppers, and I was nearly starved, and had the headache and sore feet, and was getting wet through.

" The drunken man said : ' Come and go home with me ; if the old woman gives us any of her jaw—hic— between me and you we can lick her and kick her out of doors—hic.'

" I was glad to find a place to shelter me from the storm, but of all the wretched holes I ever saw, that shanty beat. The poor, wretched woman took pity on me and let me dry my clothes and eat my supper without a word. I never ate such bread. As I worked away at it I couldn't help but think of mother's light biscuits, and I came very near bursting out crying again. I stayed all night, and after trying to eat a little more of that awful bread for breakfast I thanked them and started on my journey. I traveled until about the middle of the afternoon. By that time my feet were so sore I could scarcely walk. I sat down upon the high bank alongside the railroad and, taking off my shoes and stockings, tried to rest. A freight train dashed by. In the caboose at the end, sitting at the open window and looking out, was father. As the train passed me he was almost near enough to touch me. We looked in each other's face just a second, and the train whirled along and he was hid by a cloud of dust. What I saw in his face just broke my heart, and I started for home as fast as my poor sore feet would let me. As I limped along, around the corner a man came toward me upon a dead run. It was father. He had got off at a little side station and was after me double-quick. He did not say one word. He just opened his arms, and I opened mine, and we ran together, and for about a minute we did some tall hugging, now, I tell you. I cried and cried, until father patted me on the head and said, smiling, while the big tears ran down his face : ' Well, my son, have you had all the soldiering you want ? '

"I said : ' Yes, sir ; I want to go home.'

" We walked to the next station, and as I stood there looking through the window of a restaurant while we were waiting for the train, father said : ' I suppose hard-tack is pretty tough food for a soldier boy who is used to light biscuit; suppose you try a pie for a change.' He bought the biggest pie in the whole ranch and just laughed and cried as I ate every blessed crumb. We got on the train and came home, and that's all."

Tom's eyes were suspiciously wet, and his voice trembled a little as he said : " I'm glad it's over, Jack, and you're safe at home. It was a sorry old time when we found you had really gone. Father walked the floor all night, and mother cried herself to sleep, and I thought of all the times I had teased and bullied you, and I felt mean and sorry, I tell you ; and promised if ever you got back from war without being killed I'd let up on the nagging and joking. You won't suffer for want of it, you may be sure. The boys at school are just waiting to get hold of you. You will have to stand it and make the best of it. The first day will be a scorcher."

After several days waiting for the sore feet to get well and rested Jack started to school, determined to be brave and good-natured. He expected to have to endure every indignity that shrewd and mischievous boys could invent. He was not disappointed. Every boy was on the look-out. As soon as Jack's sturdy figure appeared in sight one crowd formed as if they were a band, and, imitating every kind of music, pretended to escort him, as if he were a distinguished stranger. The rest formed two lines, and as Jack walked between them, all shouted together, " See, the conquering hero comes ! " All the joking was taken good-naturedly until one of the larger boys, the son of the church treasurer, made an insulting remark about raising the salary of the pauper minister so that he could waste a little more on his prodigal. The stinging

taunt had hardly been spoken before Jack's hard fist
had been dashed into the jeering face. "A fight! a
fight! Let's see the soldier fight." Although Jack
was very much the smaller boy of the two, his blood
was up and he required no urging. To the amazement of all, his activity and blood-earnestness and marvelous pluck more than offset his antagonist's superior
size and strength. Jack fought as if a nation's life
depended on his victory. Utterly regardless of the
blows that fell quick and heavy upon head and
body, he clenched his burly enemy, and, being a famous
wrestler, caught him in a lock by a neat trick he had
learned, and threw him heavily. A convenient stone
received the big boy's head, and the battle was over.
Jack, feeling the strong frame which he still held in
a tight grip relax and lie still, sprang to his feet and
shouted: "I've killed him! I've killed him!"

Stooping down and trying to lift the injured boy, he
was delighted to hear a groan, which proved him not
dead, but only badly injured. Dazed and white and
weak, he tried to stand, but fell limp and faint. "I'm
whipped, boys. Served me right. Jack, forgive me '
it was all my fault."

The boys, crowd-like, shouted themselves hoarse
over Jack's victory, and were ready to crown as a
hero the unfortunate fellow whom a few minutes

before they were jeering and tormenting as an object of contempt.

Jack, panting, said, as he wiped the blood from his badly battered face : " Fellows, I was an idiot to run away from as good a home as I had. I ought to be tormented to death for it. None of you chaps can say as mean things about me as I feel. I will take any thing, but I will fight any boy, big or little, that will insult my father. I've got the best father in town. He never jawed a mite, but just hugged and kissed and forgave me. I know he's poor; but he could earn money if he wanted to. He's the strongest man in town. Bill's father is a big, strong fellow, as all blacksmiths are, but my father lifted a log the other day that Bill's father couldn't budge. Ain't that so, Bill ? "

Bill cheerily said : " Yes; father said the minister was stronger than a yoke of oxen."

" My father never went to school; but he learned himself, and he could have been a judge if he'd been a lawyer. But he became a minister because God wanted him to; and I think it's bad enough for him to have such a boy as me without being insulted for it."

The boys gave three cheers for Jack the Prodigal. A little shaver piped out : " A tiger for the Prodigal's pap," and such a groan and growl were given that you would have thought it was a whole menagerie let loose.

It required all of Jack's grit and courage to face the ridicule that the whole village poured upon him. The nickname became his common name, and he was oftener called "The Prodigal" than he was plain Jack. A short time after his return he made his first speech in meeting. The village class-leader was a pompous old fellow. He had been a class-leader for many years. He had acquired the habit of using "the holy tone" whenever he talked religion. He had a shrill, quavering sort of a voice, and when he lifted it, after the fashion of an old-time preacher he had heard in his youth, and then let it fall with wave-like regularity, always ending in a peculiar and indescribable grunt—"ah"—it was a great treat to the boys. When he "warmed up" and poured forth his exhortations and appeals and exegesis in a wonderful medley, the whole neighborhood was interested. Many young people regularly attended Methodist meeting solely in hopes to hear the good brother's sing-song address and prayer. The good leader saw in Jack's adventure a chance to point a moral for the benefit of the young people, to whom he had grown accustomed in recent years to address all his exhortations. By some good fortune the leadership of the church prayer-

112 The Pharisee and the Prodigal.

meeting was given to him, and he announced after
the sermon by the pastor that the subject would be
"The Prodigal," and he hoped the younger portion
of the community would be out. The largest attendance for many weeks was present. Tom and Jack,
unconscious of the subject, were in their places, and
by some accident sat in a part of the church separate
from all the rest and in plain view of all. When the
leader began to read with his sing-song sniffle the
story of "The Prodigal Son," Jack turned red and
white, and then, with clenched fist and tightly closed
lips, sat bolt upright and looked at the leader and
listened. The prayer began: "O thou unmerciful
God, have mercy on our dear pasture, thy unworthy
servant; bless his weak and feeble instrumentality.
Thou who canst take a worm and thrash a mountain,
make him a power in this community, as thou hast
not yet; he is wading through deep waters. Thou
hast humbled him by giving him wicked and rebell-
ious children; help him set a better example before
his own household, that they may no longer be a
reproach to thy cause in this place." And so on the
prayer ran for nearly half an hour. Tom knelt down
clear out of sight, but Jack violated all sense of pro-
priety by sitting bolt upright and looking squarely
into the face of the praying leader, with anger and

grief in turn struggling for the mastery in his little heart. The fierce struggle was written upon his chubby face by flushes and frowns and trembling lips and eyes now on fire and now wet with tears. As soon as the prayer was ended the leader began to amplify and emphasize the story he had read for a les-son. He wound up his exegesis by returning to the parsonage for a horrible illustration.

He said: "It is well known that this story—ah—has found an illustration in the home of our minister within a few weeks—ah. Ministers' families, as a rule—ah—are far from being models for the families of the parish—ah. Ministers'. children have always been known to be the worst in town—ah—but our present pasture has been unusually afflicted—ah. His youngest son, and I am glad to see him here to-night—ah—and I hope he will pay strict attention to my few and feeble remarks—ah—our minister's son, like the prodigal of the story—ah—has been gone into a far country—ah—and wasted his subsistence in righteous living—ah—and has now returned to point a moral and adorn a tale—ah."

For twenty minutes poor Jack sat and listened to the exhortations which portrayed the similarity be-tween his little trip and the journey of the prodigal. At the close the leader and the congregation were

8

electrified by seeing Jack rise and say he wanted to say a few words.

His indignation had so completely swallowed up his timidity that he spoke without a tremor and in a clear boyish treble which made the little church ring.

"I'm much obliged to the leader for holding me up as a warning and example, but I think he could have found a better one a little nearer home. His own son Jack, for instance. He ain't no prodigal, but if he should ever run away no one would be sorry, unless he came back."

This hit at the leader's scapegrace son, who was the terror and pest of the community, took away the old man's breath.

"If my father was here you all know he wouldn't 'low no such nonsense as this. Ministers' families are about as good as the average, and if the boys don't turn out as well as they might, it's because every body's pickin' and peepin' and lecturin' and scoldin'. If I was ever so sorry for what I know was wrong this kind of a meetin' 'd only make me mad and swear a good deal quicker 'n pray. I think it's bad enough for my father to work as he does here for hardly enough to live on, without havin' his family ridiculed and slandered and bein' called a worm and

a weak and feeble instrument. You all know my father ain't no weak instrument. He is the strongest
man in town. He could, if he was a mind to, take
any two men in town and thump their heads together.
He never went to school, but he learned himself and
knows more 'n all the town put together. He's the
best father in the world. When I just broke his
heart, he loved me and forgave me, and never 's
throwed it up to me once. And I am goin' to try
and be a better boy, and I hope you'll all do the
same. But I ain't comin' here to be preached at by
any body 't 'l call my father and God names. If you
want a text for your next sermon," turning to the
leader, " you might tell the people that a man 't has
a prodigal of his own 'd better let other people's
prodigals alone."

Not once did Jack waver, save when he spoke of
his father's love ; but he soon regained his nerve and
finished his speech, and while the audience sat dazed
with surprise and merriment combined, he walked
out, and the meeting broke up without another word.
None the less did Jack hear himself called every-
where and by every body, " Jack the Prodigal."

CHAPTER II.

TOM THE PHARISEE.

"TOM'S a saint, I know. He always was. He was born so. They say Christians are born again ; I will have to be born several times before I can hold a candle to my respected and perfect brother. I have heard his praise sung ever since I heard any thing. It is getting to be a little monotonous. Tom's good, and knows it. I'm bad, and every body knows it. O, dear! I wonder if I will ever be any thing but the prodigal, always in trouble and always being lectured about not being good."

"Come, Jack, get up out of bed. You sha'n't be allowed to mope any longer like this. You're in a bad scrape, I know, but then you're always in some kind of a scrape. This is a little the worst you have ever been caught in, but you'll live through it."

"There you go again, you blessed old Pharisee. I was just talking to myself about you before you came in. It is no credit to you to be good. You were born perfect. All the weaknesses you ought to have had were given to me, and all the virtues I was entitled to by some mistake were passed over to you. I wish I hadn't been born twins, and the youngest at that. Then I might have stood some show in this world. If ever I go to State's prison or am hung it will all be because I was your twin brother. It is the same old game over. I'm Esau and you're Jacob; and you have always had the advantage of me. You started a few minutes ahead, and I never can catch up. I suppose if I had had the start, as Esau had, you would still have beaten me. How does it seem to have every body singing your praise? Don't you feel like praying to yourself sometimes, or have you got beyond prayer?"

"You're getting daft as well as wicked, Jack. You can be as good as any body when you try. This wretched college scrape, that has made us all such trouble and has cost father so much money, as poorly as he can spare it, was nothing but stupid folly on your part. What business have you, who might be the best student in the college, as every body knows you are the smartest, to go knocking around with those lazy, shiftless, vulgar loafers? They sneer at you when your back is turned, and banter each other to see which can get the minister's son into the most trouble. If I had my choice, whether I'd be a Pharisee or a prodigal, I'd be a Pharisee every time. I think a good deal of the old Pharisee. He had religion and wasn't ashamed of it. Like a man, he

acknowledged his obligation to God and did not sneak
out of it. He paid tithes and gave to the poor and
prayed, and did not care who knew it. It is true he
bragged about it, but when it comes to bragging the
prodigal can give the Pharisee odds every time, and
then beat him. When a sinner turns from his sins
he seems to take delight in dragging into every body's
sight the miserable, shameful record he has made.
He boasts of how mean and cruel and foolish and
dirty he was, until it is a wonder he does not make
every one despise him. I'd be ashamed to say much
about my sins. If a man is going to boast it is more
to his credit that he boasts of being virtuous and honest and clean than that he has been dishonest, drunk-
en, and filthy. I hope when they cut an epitaph on
my tombstone they will put at the top the name you
gave me in a joke when we were boys—'Tom the
Pharisee.'"

"I'm afraid if I don't quit the prodigal business
before I die you'll have to bury me at night and without any tombstone at all," said Jack, sorrowfully. "I
wish I knew how to become better."

"Cheer up, you dear old prodigal; we will both
turn over a new leaf. I am afraid I am as much to
blame for your college scrapes as you. I did not look
after you and get you with the right kind of a crowd

when we first went to college, as I ought to have done. But when we go back I will take you under my wing; you know I'm a few minutes the older. If you will be my mentor and keep me from playing the prig and tone down a little of my Pharisaism, it will be a fair exchange."

"All right, Tom; it makes me feel better right off to hear you acknowledge that there is a possibility of improving you, and I am to be honored with having a part in the work of reform. I am afraid it will be a hard battle to get me away from the swine and husks, but I'll try if you will help."

"You must help me now," said Tom; "I'm in a scrape myself. You know I have never had very much reverence for what I thought was humbuggery or hypocrisy. I have been reading very much of late of the investigations of the higher critics concerning the authorship of the Bible, and have had my faith a little shaken. I have been a little irreverent, I fear, in my references to the Bible, especially when I have had a chance to torment some good people whom I thought were ninnies. I have had just such an adventure. You know old Brother Prosy? He was an itinerant on trial, but he could not pass the examinations and they dropped him about fifty years ago, more or less. He became a local preacher, and

is one of the kind that I like to fool with.   He and I
had a discussion about the Bible to-day, and he was
so horrified that the first chance he has in church he
will make as horrible an example of me as the old
class-leader did of you.   I have not the courage to
lay him out as you did the old leader.   I will stay away
from prayer-meeting all during the vacation until I
know that he has freed his mind.''

"Come and tell me about it," said Jack.   "It will
help me forget my troubles that are about breaking
my heart as well as splitting my head.''

"Old Brother Prosy called to see father, and as
father was not at home I was called upon to entertain him.   As I came into the parlor I had a book in
my hand.   Brother Prosy, noticing the book, said :

" 'I see you keep up your studies during your
vacation ? '

" ' Hardly,' I said ; ' I was just reading a little.'

" ' What is it ?   Some new-fangled idee, I'll vent-
ure.'

" ' Yes ; it is a book on higher criticism.'

" ' What is higher criticism ? '

" ' It is an examination of the claims of the Bible
to be an inspired book.   The author takes the ground
that the books of Moses were written by some one
else, and—'

" ' Rank infidelity !   He must be an infidel ! ' said
Brother Prosy, sharply interrupting me.

" ' No,' I said ; ' he is a good Methodist.'

" I saw I was in for it now.   The look of horror
on the old man's face was comical, and I had to
smile.

" ' I see by the way you are laughing that you are
one of them " higher critics " yourself.'

" Surprised, and thinking I would have a little
sport with the old man, I said :

" ' I lean a little that way sometimes.'

" ' Ah ! I told your father a college edication would
be the ruin of you.   Here you are only half through,
and have thrown the Bible away already.'

" Hoping to get him started on a new tack, I
said :

" ' But you know there are many things in the
Bible about which the commentaries are not agreed.'

" ' Commentaries, indeed ! What do I want with
commentaries ?   I 'low no man to chaw over the
bread of life for me.'

" ' But you know there are many passages which
scholars interpret differently, and those of us who
cannot read the Bible in the original tongue need a
little help.'

" ' Original tongue !   English is good enough for

me. I want nobody to talk to me about Greek or
Hebrew. They may be good enough for Jews or
other heathen, but I prefer a civilized language.'

" ' Must we take the literal meaning of the Bible,
then, as we have it ? '

" ' Certainly ; I believe the whole Bible is inspired,
every word ; all or none, say I.'

" ' But there are some places where the best scholars
agree that the rendering is not the exact translation.
In Genesis the word " day " really means " period;"
the meaning is that God made the world in six peri-
ods, and not in six days.'

" ' It is rank blasphemy! I suppose God knew
what he was about when he said he created the world
in six days and rested on the seventh.'

" ' But geology pretends to find evidence in the
rocks of ages of growth and decay.'

" ' I want to know if God did make the world at
all if it would not be just as easy to make it in six
minutes as in six millions of ages. Perhaps these men
that know so much might have taught him more than
he knew. It is a pity the Almighty did not have
them around.'

" ' Joshua told the sun to stand still. How would
that help him when day and night are produced by
the moving of the earth, and not the sun ? '

"'It means just what it says, and it says just what it means. Geology, geography, astronomy, grammar, or algebra, it's all one to me. If the Bible said the moon was made of green cheese, I would believe it in spite of all the astronomers that ever lived or ever will live.'

"'What about the whale swallowing Jonah? They say a whale cannot swallow a man. Its throat is so small that it is utterly impossible.'

"'Impossible! Yes, impossible with man, may be; but with God all things are possible. You need not try to shake my faith, my boy. I am so well grounded that if the Bible had said Jonah swallowed the whale, it wouldn't make me tremble a second. I'd believe it just as quick. One is just as easy to do as the other, perhaps; it makes no difference.'

"'May it not be that in copying the Bible they made some mistakes?'

"'No! If God inspired men to write the book, he could inspire men to copy it.'

"'But the translators might have made mistakes.'

"'They were inspired.'

"'The printers often make mistakes.'

"'They will be inspired.'

"'Then you are not in favor of revising the Bible.'

"'No, sir! It would be a terrible sacrilege. You

know what is said about him that taketh from or addeth to the word of God?'

"'I was reading a book the other day which greatly interested me. The author was one of the most distinguished men in the Church. He said that man was naturally mortal; he does not die because of sin; death is a part of God's economy just as much as life.'

"'All the fools are not dead yet,' said the old man.

"'But let us look at it and see,' said I. 'Suppose nobody had ever died!'

"'I know what you are coming at! There would have been plenty of room.'

"'Let us figure it out and see! Suppose every married pair had had four children and none had died?'

"'Four is too small a family; give them each as many as Jacob had.'

"'We will try four first and see how it comes out.'

"'Well, go ahead,' said the old man; 'I know what you are after; but I tell you before you begin, I'm too well grounded to be upset by any new theology.'

"'There have been about two hundred generations since Adam. If each married couple had had four children, and none had died, there would have been three octillions of decillions of people.'

" ' Yes ; I suppose there would have been as many as that,' said Brother Prosy, with a wise look and nod of the head.

" ' We will divide the earth's surface up into square feet, and give every person one square foot.'

" ' That is not enough; give them an acre at least, there is plenty of land.'

" ' We will start with a square foot and see how the land will hold out. If we divide the number of people by the number of square feet, we will find that there are five hundred billions of decillions of persons to each square foot.'

" Old Brother Prosy gasped, and began to rub his head and stare at me as if he were losing his reason. I went on :

" ' In order to give each one his foot of space, we will stand the people on each other's shoulders and call their average height four feet.'

" ' Yes,' murmured Brother Prosy.

" ' We would have every foot of the earth's surface covered by a column of people four hundred millions of decillions of miles high. How near the sun do you suppose the top man would be ? ' I asked, in order to give him a moment to breathe.

" ' I hardly know,' he said, a little bewildered. ' I suppose near enough to be uncomfortably warm.'

"'The topmost man would be four decillion times
as far away as the sun.   As it takes eight minutes for
a ray of light to come from the sun to the earth, if
we had an express train to travel as fast as light does
it would take the lowest man fifty octillions of years
to get to the topmost man.'

"Utterly bewildered, the old man said, under his
breath, 'If Eve had not eaten the apple we would
have been in a terrible fix.   At least those at the bottom would.'   After meditating for a moment, he said,
'What do you call this?'

"I said : 'The author does not give it any name, but
I suppose we might call it "mathematical theology."'

"'More like diabolical theology.   I want you to
know I'm too deeply grounded in my religion to be
upset by any new theology, whether it's mathematical
or diabolical.   If I was your father I'd set you to
learning a trade instead of filling your head with that
sort of nonsense.   And this is what you call higher
criticism.   I have wondered why your father seemed
to have so much anxiety.   It is bad enough to have a
prodigal scapegrace to scandalize and bankrupt him
with his college scrapes, but that's a mercy to having
a son of prayer become a son of perdition, as I believe
all infidels are, whether they are critics of the high
church or the low church.   All are of the devil, and

will have their part in the lake of fire and brimstone.'
And he stormed out."

"Good for Brother Prosy," said Jack. "He served
you right. You are trying to excuse your sins by picking flaws in the Bible, and I excuse mine by picking
flaws in Christians. We are both in mighty mean
business. You are a higher critic and I am a hypercritic. I am afraid both words could be spelled the same
way and truly applied to us both—H-y-p-o-c-r-i-t-i-c."

CHAPTER III.

THE HIGHER CRITIC AND THE HYPERCRITIC.

TOM and Jack both graduated, and each had begun
what promised to be a remarkable career. Tom
was a professor in a leading college, and his brilliant
pen was never busy enough to supply the demand
from the best periodicals of the land. He had never
cast aside the nominal faith of his father, and was still
a Methodist in name. But he had imbibed all the
daring notions of the so-called higher critics concerning the Bible while claiming still to be an orthodox
believer. He was the center of life of a large club of
brilliant men, and had inspired a multitude of young
men to accept his leadership in biblical criticism, and

in every single instance their criticism had been destructive of all faith in the supernatural of the Bible or belief in its inspiration.

Jack studied medicine and discovered his mission the hour he entered the medical college. He became at the very start a wonderfully skillful surgeon. The faculty said : " He is born to be a surgeon, and would outstrip us all were he as steady as he is skillful." He was still the same prodigal, warm-hearted, impulsive, social, but his own worst enemy. He was not addicted to the use of strong drink. He valued his standing too highly to risk the loss of his firm hand and steady nerve, which he knew drink was sure to destroy. He was wild, reckless, and in a fair way to become wicked. After completing his medical education he became a member of the faculty, and soon secured a position upon the staff of one of the leading hospitals.

He was sitting in his room one night after a singularly novel and successful surgical operation which was destined to make him famous. The reaction from the highly wrought tension of nerve occasioned by the serious character of the operation just completed brought upon him one of the despondent, gloomy conditions of mind in which he had several times taken to drink. He was about to ring a bell and order a bottle of brandy when a letter was brought by a special delivery messenger. As he broke the seal the clock struck twelve. The letter was from Tom. It was very brief:

"DEAR OLD PRODIGAL: As I was looking over some of father's papers I found the inclosed letter addressed to you and sealed. I was greatly startled. I had looked these papers over scores of times before, and could not understand how it could have escaped my attention. It must have slipped inside another letter. It seemed so much a special message from our dear father who has been dead so many years that I send it by special delivery. Yours lovingly,   TOM."

Jack held the letter in his hand several minutes before he opened it. All the past rushed before him in panoramic form. His father's patient, heroic self-sacrifice for his family and his Church, which had never been understood by the boy, now became so real to the man that he bowed his head and sobbed. His own life from boyhood to young manhood stood before him as if he were watching the life-story of another acted out before him. His father's tender devotion and loving forgiveness and his own thoughtlessness and recklessness made the strong man shed many bitter tears. After he had grown calm he opened the letter. The familiar hand-writing startled him.

9

It was impossible that the hand that penned this letter looking so fresh and clear had been hidden under the sod for so many years. The letter was not long. One reading fastened it in his memory so that he would remember every word and line :

"DEAR JACK : To-day the physician told me I must die. I knew it before, and was not surprised at all. I shall never see you again in this world. Before you can reach me I will be dead. My first thought was you, my prodigal boy. I think I love you better than Tom because you have made me more trouble than he. I write this as my last earthly word to you. I charge you as a dying man not to cheat me out of your presence in heaven. I do not know what heaven will be, but it cannot be the same to me without you. My family must be unbroken, or heaven will not be heaven to me. You have been a wild and reckless but good-hearted boy; you are now a wild and reckless man—must I say it?—I fear you are a wicked young man. If you die in your sins you will go to hell. Jack, my boy, if it were in my power to go to hell in your stead, how gladly would I do it! I cannot. I pray now that God will make these words of your dying father the words of God to you. Promise me you will meet me in heaven. O God! I have tried all these years to save this boy that thou hast given me ; for thy Son's sake, save my son."

The letter stopped abruptly, and the firm hand-writing became an almost illegible scrawl before it ended. Jack read it through with a glance that seemed to devour it in an instant. Utterly over-whelmed, he dropped the letter and fell upon his knees in an anguish of soul that could not be voiced. He thought he heard that voice he remembered so well repeating over and over, "O God ! for thy Son's sake, save my son." It was repeated, sounding fainter and fainter, like a dying echo. Filled with terror lest the prayer should cease and be lost, he cried, "O God ! for my father's sake, save me !" He had scarcely uttered the sentence before the room was filled with heavenly light and a voice said to him : "Thy sins are forgiven thee; go and sin no more." He sang and shouted nearly all night. Those who were near enough to hear the noise, but unable to dis-tinguish its character, said, as they turned over in their beds : " It's that mad-cap doctor having another spree. Too bad ! Too bad !"

The first mail brought a letter from the chief surgeon in the hospital with which Jack was con-nected. It was very brief.

"My Dear Doctor: I have just received an application from a hospital in Japan for a surgeon-in-chief. You fill the bill exactly with one exception—they must have a Christian. The salary will be less than half what we pay you, but it is an opportunity for a Christian that comes but once in a life-time. My first thought was that you were the man God wants for Japan. Your father and I were old friends. Were he living he would say the call of Japan is the voice of God. As surgeon-in-chief in this hospital seeking you you can do more good than twenty missionaries. The surgeon must go in the first steamer. Come and see me immediately."

Before accepting the invitation of his chief he telegraphed Tom:

"Miracles have not ceased. Father's letter was the voice of God. Jesus has saved me from my sins, blessed be his name! Come at once and bid me good-bye. I am going to Japan as a medical missionary in the first steamer. Jack."

Tom, thinking Jack was crazy, took the first train. He found him in his right mind and as happy as he could be.

"What does this mean, Jack? Are you really going

to give up your brilliant position here to become a missionary in Japan?"

"Yes, old fellow; I have heard God speak. I dare not disobey. I never knew what enjoyment was before. I would walk into an open grave with a shout, if he wanted me to. I now understand how our father endured the privations of the itinerancy. I used to get vexed and cross and almost impudent trying to urge him to quit preaching and turn to some profession that would give him a comfortable living. He would simply smile, and say, 'My dear Jack, when God speaks to you it will be easy to obey. I would not exchange my work of preaching Christ to become a king.' I thought then he was crazy, just as you think I am crazy now. I should not be a bit surprised if God would speak to you some day, and you would take the first steamer to Japan, to help me in my work or take it up when I lay it down; who knows? Tom, never forget that father did not think he needed to write you. He counted you already saved. I fear if you ever were a Christian, when you lost faith in the inspiration of the Bible, every thing else went with it. I am bound to meet father and mother. What an awful thing it would be if when I got there father should say, 'Where's Tom?' Don't cheat him out of the joy he counted so sure."

Tom promised that he would meet Jack and his father and mother in heaven. As the vessel sailed out, Tom waved his handkerchief, and said, "Good-bye, dear Jack!" Jack replied, "Good-bye, dear Tom, remember!"

CHAPTER IV.

LETTER FROM NEW YORK.

THE rest of our story is obtained from several letters written from New York to Japan and replies to the same. The correspondents were twin brothers, the sons of a wealthy and cultured nobleman. One of the brothers was making an extended journey through the world, studying the civilizations and religions of the various countries. He had been in America several months, and was residing in New York at the time the following letter was written:

"MY DEAR BROTHER: As you know, I have been studying the many religions of this strange country. I try to attend all of the great religious gatherings. I attended the meetings of the American Board of Foreign Missions to-day. At first I was very sorry, but at last was greatly delighted. I listened with painful interest to a paper on Japan. It was prepared by the missionaries of the Christian religions now trying to delude our people. The paper spoke of their success in leading our people from their ancestral faith, and urged that more missionaries be sent with money to buy converts.

"If our people could only visit America and see what I see every day, we would not need to worry much over their becoming converts to Christianity. If they could see the drunkenness and shameless vice, the desecration of the Christian's holy day, and the disregard for the Christian's holy book, they would be in no great hurry to become Christians. Very few of the Christian temples are more than half full, while the saloons, which I understand are the temples of the enemies of the Christian religion, are always crowded. I supposed, from hearing the Christian missionaries in our country, that all educated and holy people were devotees of the Christian religion. But I find that a very large number of the best and wisest people treat all religions with the greatest disrespect and contempt. Indeed, many of them do not seem to do any thing else but try to overthrow the Christian religion. As I came out of the great church in which the missionary meeting was held a paper was handed me which was called the *Christian Union.* I have read it carefully and have found in it what I long have sought. The Christians have a little book containing questions and answers about their religion which they use in instructing their children. They call this little book a catechism. I found in the *Christian Union* some questions and answers about a new religion which seemed to me like a catechism. I asked a wise literary man what kind of a catechism it was.

"He said : ' It must be the catechism of the Higher Criticism.'

"His words were very strange. I had never heard before that there was a religion called the Higher Criticism. I determined to investigate it, and if possible obtain a copy of the catechism. It is just what we need to have translated into our language to prevent our people from becoming seduced into the acceptance of the Christian religion. I did not investigate very far before I was filled with joy. The teachings of the new religion are as full of superstitions and foolish doctrines as the old, but they completely overthrow the old. As we desire to defeat the missionaries, this new religion appears to be the very instrument we need. I know nothing about the new religion but what its devotees have told me. It is, as near as I can learn, an improvement upon the old faiths. The higher critic is an honest Christian. He confesses what all other intelligent Christians know and believe but dare not acknowledge. He discards very much, if not all, of the supernatural portions of the holy book. He spends his time seeking out new flaws and discrediting more wonders. When he has accomplished his desires, all the miraculous portions of the holy book will be proved to be fabulous, and must be rejected by all honest and intelligent minds.

"As this is a very strange matter, and hard for us to understand, I can make it plain to you by quoting a few questions and answers which are published in the *Christian Union*, October 17, 1889. This will give you an idea what kind of a book this new catechism is, and how important it is that we shall at once procure it for our people. These questions seem to be from persons who are studying the new religion and desire more light. The answers are from the teachers or priests of the new faith :

"'QUESTION.—I have much use for the story of Eden as an allegory, but if I must regard it as actual history or be cast out as an unbeliever, I shall take to the woods. What say you?

"'ANSWER.—We do not think that you will be disturbed. Even conservative scholars now hold the view that the early part of Genesis contains some "spiritualized legends."'

"This question and answer cost me a great deal of study. I could not understand why the questioner should 'take to the woods,' and what good it would do him if he did. But at last I learned that here was a truth absolutely invaluable to us. You will remember that the missionary begins his work by telling our people that they are sinners—that in Eden our forefather was tempted by an evil spirit in the form of a serpent and led to disobey the Christian's God. Because men became sinners God was incarnated in Jesus and died to save them. You can easily see that if the story of Eden is a legend, to publish that fact will spoil lots of sermons for the missionaries. Besides, Jesus speaks of this legend, as a historic fact. This makes him either ignorant or untruthful. In either case he is unfit to save us; he would better save himself. There can be no mistake about this story being a legend, for 'conservative scholars'—those who oppose the Higher Criticism—now acknowledge that 'it is but an allegory.'

"'Q.—As the world was not created in six days, how could the Sabbath have been instituted by God on the ground that he had rested on the seventh day, as stated in the fourth commandment? Do you believe that the commandments and all the laws in the Pentateuch were given by God, or written by Moses?

" ' A.—Many of them proceeded from Moses's successors building on to his work, and so were only involved in, or developed from, what the " Lord said to Moses." What God said to Moses he probably communicated, as now to us, inwardly, by enlightening the mind and conscience to see the truth and feel its imperativeness. The Sabbath is of divine appointment—" made for man," as Jesus says—required by the physical and moral nature which God made. That Moses should see this law written in our nature and assign a fanciful reason for it only shows that he was like the rest of us in being better able to see what is right than to give a reason for it.'

"I could hardly believe this when I read it. I had believed the missionaries to be honest but misguided men. I admired their heroism in leaving their native land to teach us what they called a better religion. I fear I must now believe them to be wicked deceivers. Let me just put into a few words the things they have taught us which are untrue :

" ' Moses taught the people the law of God and gave them his commandments written upon tables of stone.' This is a legend. Many commandments have been added to those which Moses gave ; indeed, Christians are not sure that Moses wrote any part of the holy book, or gave any part of the law; it may be that Moses himself is a myth.

" 'Moses talked with God face to face,' the missionaries said; but the fact is, God talked to Moses just as he talks to every body, by enlightening the mind and conscience.

" 'The Sabbath is God's day; God worked six days, and rested the seventh, and hallowed it.' This is another legend—ought I not to say a lie? Moses saw the benefit of resting one day in seven, and gave as a 'fanciful reason' for its observance that God ordained it.

" There are other questions and answers just as important to us as those I have already given.

" ' Q.—Kindly answer for me a few questions on 1 Sam. xv, 2, 3. Did God give the command there recorded? If he did, did he not command to do a cruel and wicked deed from revengeful motives? If he did not, and Samuel and the author of the Book of Samuel supposed that he did, is not their mistake about the character and dealings of God so serious as to render them untrustworthy teachers of religious truth?'

" I read that question over twice before I read the answer. It sounded very much like a little book called *The Mistakes of Moses*, written by a lawyer who is a very funny fellow. He charges Christians fifty cents to let them hear him make fun of their holy book. Instead of treating this question with indignation and rebuking the questioner, the teacher answers it as if it were a perfectly proper and respectful question.

" ' A.—The passage evidently enjoins retaliation for hostilities four hundred years past. The war (on banditti) was probably justifiable. The motive appealed to (revenge) was not. The phrase "Thus saith the Lord" does not necessarily denote a direct divine command. Compare 2 Sam. xvi, 10. It often means no more than "It is right," or "It ought to be." In any case, it shows, as here used, a defective moral judgment, and that Samuel's teachings, like those of all the other saints, must be brought before the judgment-seat of Christ for revision and correction. It is only fair to notice other occasions on which Samuel taught moral truths that are quite up to the principle of Christ.

" ' Q.—How would the Higher Criticism dispose of the shadow going back ten degrees in the sun-dial of Ahaz ? (2 Kings xx.)

" ' A.—A similar phenomenon was observed in 1703 by the prior of Metz. By a peculiar refraction of solar light the shadow of the sun-dial went back an

hour and a half.   It has been suggested that the
sign may have been due to the shadow-movement in
a solar eclipse which was visible at Jerusalem Jan-
uary 11, B. C. 689.   This, under certain conditions,
would recede with regular motion for twenty minutes
time.'

"As you will see by reading the holy book, Ahaz
wanted a sign that he would recover from his illness.
Isaiah, one of the holy men, gave him his choice, ' to
have the shadow go forward or backward on the sun-
dial.'   Ahaz said, 'It would be a little thing for the
shadow to go forward; let it go backward ten degrees.'   Isaiah prayed to his God, and he brought the
shadow ten degrees backward.   Our people are too
shrewd to be caught by such a trick as that.   If this
going backward of the shadow was simply owing to
a natural cause, Isaiah must have known it.   Then he
too is an impostor.   If he knew that an eclipse was
going to make the shadow go backward, for him to
pretend to pray to his God to make it go back, and
then declare that the turning back was an answer
to his prayer, proves that he was not only a wicked
deceiver of his king, but that he was guilty of sacrilege
by making his God an accomplice in his trick.   I do
not know when I was happier than when I read these
questions and answers.   I saw immediately of what

vast importance they would be to us in our work of stemming the tide toward the Christian's religion in our beloved Japan.

" There is one story in the holy book that the missionaries never tire talking about. The first time I heard it I was deeply moved. The missionary was a very eloquent man. He described the scene in a powerfully dramatic manner. I almost imagined I heard the great general command the sun and moon to stand still. When the missionary assured us that God heard the prayer of his servant and made the sun and moon obey him, and this incident was recorded to show us that God was always willing to do wonderful things when his servants called upon him, I wished for a moment that I had such a God as that. What must I think of the honesty or intelligence of that missionary? His wonderful story is the make-believe of some romancer. When I read this question and answer I sprang to my feet and shouted aloud: 'The missionary was a liar, and I will hunt the world over till I find him and tell him so.'

" ' Q.—I understand the Higher Criticism to dispose of the matter of Joshua's commanding the sun to stand still by resolving it into a poetic fiction?

" ' A.—Substantially. It is, on the face of it, quoted from a poetical book. Orthodox interpreters now

recognize this. The fact that Joshua addresses the
moon also, though before sunset it could give no light,
leads to the same conclusion.'

" You will not at first see the full significance of
this truth which we have just learned. Two of the
holy men called prophets, Isaiah and Habakkuk, who
helped write the holy book, refer to this incident as
actually occurring. If they were prophets, and by a
strange endowment of wisdom from the gods could
foretell coming events, how could they be kept in
ignorance of events that had already transpired ? If
they were not ignorant—and it does not seem possible
that their God would permit them to mix fables with
their sublime predictions—then they perpetrated a
fraud by recording as history what they knew was
' poetic fiction.' As you will remember that Isaiah
was the same holy man who played the sun-dial trick
on King Ahaz, it is not at all surprising that he should
prove to be a deceiver in another sun-story. You
will see the full force of this when you remember
that it is Isaiah who prophesies about Christ, and de-
scribes him and his work and character so graphically
that some really allege that his prophecy was written
after Christ had come. It does seem as if our gods
put it into my heart to go to this great Christian
meeting. I have been shown this simple but certain

method of saving our people from the wiles of the
Christian missionaries. Does not your heart respond
to mine ?   Just think of the discomfiture of the missionaries when we put into their hands this catechism
and ask them to expound it in their public meetings.
Let me put together the untruths which these men
have taught our people as the word of God.

" The story of Eden, the fall of man, the tempta-
tion by the serpent, is a ' spiritualized legend.' The law
was not given in God's hand-writing on stone tablets.
The law was not given to Moses at all.   The Sabbath
was not instituted by divine command.   The Pentateuch is not the work of Moses written under divine
inspiration, it is a compilation of legends and poetry
and fabulous history.   Isaiah and Habakkuk per-
petrate a fraud by recording as history a piece of
poetic fiction ; Samuel was morally defective ; Isaiah
deceived Ahaz by the sun-dial trick and insulted his
God by pretending the trick was an answer to prayer ;
and, last and best of all, Jesus, who was continually
appealing to these very legends, poetic fictions, and
fabulous histories in support or illustration of his own
teaching, is also proved to be a deceiver.   He is either
grossly ignorant or deliberately untruthful.   However
we may excuse him through charity, he is certainly so
unreliable that we can accept nothing he says without
10

corroborative evidence. This Higher Criticism catechism we must have. It will rout and utterly overwhelm the wicked men who for some selfish purpose teach our people lies and deceive them by tricks in order to delude them into giving up their ancient faith. I will advertise in the *Christian Union* this week for the catechism. We will put a copy into the schools and homes of Japan, and our own holy religion will be safe."

CHAPTER V.

LETTER FROM JAPAN.

"DEAR BROTHER: Your letter was read with great joy. The copy of the *Christian Union* which you sent me I used immediately. I spoiled a sermon and broke up a Christian meeting, and sent the missionary home in tears. It was a great victory. You have been inspired by our gods to discover the very thing we need to overthrow this new religion and save our people from becoming deluded by it. When the catechism comes and we can get it printed in our own language we will be safe from this snare. But I know you are anxious to hear how I defeated the missionary. I attended the Christian meeting.

The attendance was very large. The missionary is an eloquent speaker and a wonderfully brilliant man. He is as holy as he is wise. I was very sorry to take such an advantage of him. He is perfectly honest and sincere, and could be one of the most successful of men in his own land. For him to come to our land to lead us out of the darkness of heathenism is the work of a hero; it would not be irreverent to say it is the work of a god. But he is deluded, and because he is so good and brave and kind he is all the more dangerous. His sermon, as the Christians call their ministers' addresses, was an explanation of the words from their holy book, ' The law was given by Moses, but grace and truth came by Jesus Christ.'

" The sermon was thrillingly eloquent, and the large company of our young men who were present were deeply moved. After the sermon the missionary did as he was accustomed to do. He said, ' If any desire to ask any questions I will be pleased to answer them, if I am able.'

" I had taken the precaution, by bribing the servant, to find out whether or not the missionary received this paper called the *Christian Union.* You can imagine my joy when I found that the very same copy you sent me was upon his table but had not yet been opened. I arose and said I desired to say a few words. 'Before I ask a few questions I want to tell you what my brother in New York writes me. He says that America, from which this missionary came, while it is called a Christian land, is one of the most wicked countries upon the face of the earth. The great majority of the people are indifferent to the Christian religion. Very many people, and they are respectable, educated, and many of them wealthy, are enemies of this religion and do all they can to destroy it. The churches are only half filled, while the saloons, which I understand are the temples of the enemies of religion, are crowded. The saloons are more powerful than the churches and have more votaries. The holy day is not regarded by the Christians themselves. The holy book from which the missionary preaches, and which he tells us is the word of God, is not believed to be divine by vast multitudes of educated and religious people. I now wish to ask the missionary whether or not there is a religious paper published in his country called the *Christian Union*, and what is its standing and character; who is its editor, and is it ever sent to Japan?' He answered me so promptly I knew he had not seen the paper, and I was very sorry for him. He said: 'I see the paper called the *Christian Union* every week. It is a great **paper**, with a wide circulation. Its writers are wise and good men. The editor is the pastor of one of the greatest Christian churches in America. He has long been an expounder of the holy book, and his words are quoted as those of one of the wisest and best Christian teachers.'

"I continued: 'You have spoken many times in your sermons about Eden and the fall of man through the deception of a serpent possessed by an evil spirit; this is all an allegory or fable. You have told us in this very eloquent sermon to which we have listened with so great interest that "the law was given by Moses, while grace and truth came by Jesus Christ." Of course, if one statement is not true, neither is the other. You told us about the wonderful manner in which the law was given to Moses by the gods; all this is untrue. The book you call Moses's book was written many hundreds of years after Moses was dead; it is an imposture. You have told us about a General Joshua making the sun stand still; that is a fragment of an old poem and is a romance. You told us not long ago that a king named Ahaz was sick and a prophet called Isaiah gave him as a sign that he would get well that the shadow of the sun should go back upon the sun-dial. That was only a make-believe miracle; it has occurred since, and there was nothing supernatural about it at

all. Isaiah, the holy man who played this trick, is
the one who so beautifully and truthfully described
the coming of Jesus hundreds of years before Jesus
was born. Perhaps Isaiah's prophecy was written
like Moses's law, many hundred years after he was
dead.'

"I insisted that the missionary should send to his
own house and get his copy of the *Christian Union*
and read for us certain questions and answers. He
did so, and you can never imagine the sorrowful tone
with which he read. I then addressed the audience
and said : ' You see this young man is either deceived
or is a deceiver. If he knew these things he has
tried to delude us. If he did not know them he is
unfit to be a religious teacher ; he needs instruction
himself.' The audience dispersed, laughing heartily
over my victory. As I went out I heard the missionary say to himself: ' That is the way it has
always been ; the cause of Christ has suffered more
from its friends than from its enemies.' He went
home bitterly weeping. I am anxiously waiting for
the new catechism. Send it at the earliest possible
moment."

CHAPTER VI.

LETTER FROM NEW YORK.

"DEAR BROTHER: I found I was mistaken about the new catechism. I advertised every-where for a copy, but failed to find it. I have done better. I have had one written and send you the manuscript in this mail. It is compiled from the writings of the devotees of this new faith. To my great surprise, when I began to investigate I found two kinds of higher critics. One party, which is called 'the destructive critics,' are practically infidels, as the Christians call the rejectors of the religion of Jesus. The destructive critics do not believe in the supernatural. They say no evidence is sufficient to prove a miracle. All their investigations start out by assuming that every thing that claims to be supernatural is untrue. They treat the Christian's holy book as some barbarous medicine-men among the Christians treat animals. They cut them to pieces while they are yet alive. They call it vivisecting. This party of the critics have neither pity nor regard for the holy book. They vivisect it. I was amazed when I began to

read their works. While professing to be Christians
they treated the holy book with such irreverence and
disrespect that I believed them haters of the Christian
religion rather than its devotees. Assuming that
every thing that is supernatural is fabulous, they do
not try to disprove it. They say of each miracle,
'That is a legend,' or 'It is poetry,' or 'It is an allegory' As I cannot hope to investigate for myself I
quote from them, and, as you see, this catechism spoils
nearly every wonderful story the missionary ever has
told. I found another kind of higher critics, called
'the orthodox.' They profess to have great reverence
for the holy book. They assert that their purpose is
to purify the sacred truth by separating from it legend
and tradition and fable. They seemed to wish to be
known as believers in the holy book while throwing
discredit upon it. They reminded me of the medi-
cine-man who loved his old mother, but wanted to
vivisect her when he could not get a dog. I was
greatly disappointed at finding two sects of higher
critics. I had hoped that they would be all agreed.
But after I had read many of the works of the
'orthodox critics' I found that, as far as they went,
they were just like the destructives. For the most
part they were but feeble copies or imitations of the
destructives. They were as dangerous to their own

holy book as they dared be. Both sects used the same methods and accomplished the same results ; the destructives only went a little farther, that was all the difference. I was satisfied that in time the orthodox would all become destructives. I did not have much sympathy with the reverence of the ' orthodox critics ' for the holy book. What I wanted was to get something to help me to destroy it. If they would only do that they might love it as much as they pleased. You will see that all answers are denials or assertions. I have been much impressed with this peculiarity of this new faith. Its devotees are all wise men, and know it. They think that they are authority upon all these matters. It is only necessary for them to assert or deny ; that settles all controversy. Their greatest argument is, ' We, ourselves, have said it.'

" I have had one very strange experience. After I had accumulated the matter by long and patient research I asked one wise man to recommend me to a learned literary man who would put this material into proper form, so as to make all parts harmonize. I was introduced to a brilliant professor in one of the greatest Christian colleges. He was deeply interested when I told him that I had collected from very many of the higher critics their opinions concerning the inspiration and authorship of the Christian's holy book,

and the supernatural incidents it related. He complimented me on my patience and impartiality. I
spent several days with him. He arranged the questions and answers and revised all the quotations, and
gave the little book such a wonderful beauty and
finish that I was impressed with his great ability and
learning. When it was all completed I said : ' I can
see now that for very much of the power and useful-
ness of this wonderful work I am indebted to you. I
would like to secure your services in my land to teach
my people the truths of this book. I can pledge
you a large salary. I know that with your help we
can drive the Christian religion out of my country.'
Very quickly he said :

" ' I could not do that, for I am a Christian myself. My father was a Christian minister, and I
would be very sorry to have this book used against
the Christian religion. Where do you intend to
use it ? '

" ' In Japan ; that is my native country.'

" He turned as white as a dead man, and said : ' I
wish I had known that. I will pay you any price
you may ask for this little catechism.' When I refused, he was very greatly agitated. I thought he
was going to faint. He pled with me, with tears
in his eyes, not to publish the little book. When I

left him he was walking the floor and wringing his hands. I heard him say: ' Dear Jack, how I have hurt your great, warm, loving heart.' "

CHAPTER VII.

LETTER FROM JAPAN.

" DEAR BROTHER: Your letter with the manuscript of the catechism was promptly received. I did not publish the catechism; I burned it. I have become a Christian myself, and I hope you will do the same. I know you will be greatly surprised, and, I expect, very angry. But you are a reasonable man. You know that I am not easily deluded. You believe me to be honest and sincere. Before you rashly judge me let me give you a statement of what has occurred.

"I carefully studied the catechism. The more I examined it the less I liked it. The language was elegant; as a work of literary art it was matchless. I had never seen or read any thing to compare with it. But mere denial does not disprove ; mere assertion does not establish. I searched in vain for one single argument; I found none. I searched for one single word of evidence in proof of the very strange

statements the little book contained; I found none.
The scholars of our land are not accustomed to deal
with great questions in that way. If I have no evidence in proof of these denials of the wonders of the
holy book, how do I know but the wonders are true
and the denials themselves are fables? To discredit
facts because of a fancied difference in the terms
used to describe them, or because of varying excellence of literary merit or finish in the style of the
narrator of the history, is hardly becoming wise and
scholarly men.   We can never defeat the missionaries by appealing to a trick of rhetoric or by the
mere denial or assertion of some wise man of whom
we know nothing. I determined to study the holy
book for myself. If the higher critics are right, I
can detect this weakness in the book as well as they.
I read it through carefully and critically. I found in it
many strange things recorded; but when I tried to say,
'These things are fables,' I asked myself, 'What evidence have I that they are fables?' It is not fair to
begin the examination of a wonderful thing by declar-
ing before I have seen it that there can be no wonderful thing. Because these things are wonderful is no
reason that they are incredible. If the gods wished
for any purpose to work a miracle, they would not be
the all-powerful gods if they could not do so.   It

would seem to be proper that any communication from the gods to men would be accompanied with wonders and miracles. I was compelled to believe at the start in my investigations that nothing could rightfully claim to be from the gods unless accompanied with what to me would be supernatural. Next, I asked who relate these wonderful things? I saw that they were good, pure, and holy men. From the words of deep wisdom they spoke I was convinced that they were not ignorant men. I have spent many years in the examination of the literature of many lands, and I think I know something of literary art and excellence. I found myself stopping and reading over and over the words of wisdom of the holy book and saying, 'These are the words of the gods; men, however wise, could never speak these words of their own knowledge or wisdom. I know that the men who wrote this holy book must have been men filled with all the wisdom of the gods.' When I asked, 'What in this book impresses me most?' I answered immediately, 'Character.' The men who spoke or wrote were holy men. They always advocated righteousness and denounced wickedness. Then I could not but believe if good and wise men, in order to teach men how to be holy and happy and useful, would relate wonderful things to cause men to believe they

were the messengers of the gods, the wonders must
be true.   After I had satisfied myself by my critical
study of the book that it was a credible book, given
to man to help him to be holy and pure like the
gods, I read it again to see if I could get a clew to its
real meaning.   I saw, as if it had been a puzzle picture whose key I had discovered, that every thing in
the book pointed to Jesus.   I was fascinated with
this secret truth, and read book after book to find
Jesus in it.   I saw him in the promises made to the
faithful in the early times ; then the wonderful ritual
and ceremony and law all seemed to be - finger-boards
pointing toward him.   The raptures of the prophets
sounded like the ejaculations of the heralds announcing the speedy coming of a king.   When I came to
the story of Jesus I read with a warm heart and often
with wet eyes.   My soul bowed down before this
wonderful man, who was a God as well as a man.
His life and words and death and resurrection all
seemed so fitting that I was not surprised.   It was
just what any body might have expected.   Then
those wonderful letters of the wise men who were
his followers brought to man in a simple, practical
manner all the truth of Jesus.   When I came to the
last book my soul was full of sympathy with the
wonderful story.   I saw mysteries too deep for man

only hinted at, and yet all suggesting the greatest of all mysteries—the God-man, Jesus. I closed the book in raptures. This is just such a book as the gods would write if they desired to communicate with man.

"Just at this time I became acquainted with a medical missionary. I was taken seriously ill, and for many days was near to death. When I became conscious, after many days of delirium, I saw a Christian missionary sitting by my side. I learned that he was a doctor who had been working many cures which seemed like miracles to our doctors. When our wisest doctors said I must die the Christian came and offered to take care of me. For many days he had never left my side, save for a few moments. He had saved my life, and I was very grateful. When I became strong enough to talk I asked him why he had been so kind to one who was a stranger and a heathen. He said : 'I did it for Jesus's sake.' I said : 'I have read the Christian's holy book a great deal lately and I have been very much interested in Jesus. I wish I had lived when he was on the earth ; I would like to have seen him and talked with him.'

"The missionary smiled, and said : 'He is on the earth now. I talk with him every day.'

"I could not understand him, yet I saw he was in earnest and waited for him to explain.

" He said : ' My father was a Christian minister. I
was a wicked prodigal and was a great sinner. Jesus
called me, and I heard him and obeyed him. He
saved me from my sins, and I promised him that I
would go anywhere he wanted me to go and
do any thing he commanded. He said : " Go to
Japan." I came to Japan. He told me to go about
among your people and minister to them in his name.
I came here to help you because I knew it would
please Jesus. He is my Saviour. I love him and
would be glad to die for him. He died for me.'

" My heart gave a great leap. I found myself
wishing that Jesus was my friend. I said : 'Tell me
more about Jesus.'

" He took out of his pocket a little book called the
Life of Jesus and read to me for a long time. Then
he talked about him as men talk about a dear friend
with whom they are well acquainted. The more he
talked the more I wished I had such a friend. One
day, as he was reading to me, I stopped him, and
asked :

" ' Where is Jesus now ?   I would like to have
him for my friend.'

" He said : ' He is here now,' and, smiling, he
kneeled down and began to talk with Jesus as if he
were standing by his side.

"I closed my eyes, and it seemed to me as if some one was near me. My heart was strangely moved.

"When I had fully recovered I thought of the catechism, and decided to ask the missionary's opinion of it. The next time he came to see me I asked him to look at a little book which my brother had sent me to publish and scatter in Japan to prevent our people from becoming Christians.

"He took it, and after reading a few sentences stopped, and, speaking very quickly, said, 'Who wrote this?'

"I told him it was compiled from many Christian writers and prepared in its present form for my brother by a very wise and literary man in America. I then gave him your last letter. He was greatly agitated at something in the letter. I heard him say to himself, as if greatly hurt: 'O, Tom! dear Tom! has it come to this?' He then read the catechism through very carefully. He returned it to me with a look of sadness on his face that greatly grieved me.

"'Why are you so sorry? Are these things not true?'

"He spoke very emphatically:

"'They are not true. They are but the imaginations of proud and wicked hearts.'

"I was told a few days later that the missionary

11

was very sick. I went to see him. As soon as I entered his room I felt he would die. He was very white and weak, but seemed very happy.

"He said to me: 'I am going to Jesus.'

"I said: 'I hope you will not die.'

"He quickly replied: 'Jesus said, "He that believeth in me shall never die; but if he die, yet shall he live again." Before I die I wish you would let Jesus be your Saviour.'

" I said: 'I would if I knew how.'

" He asked me to read from the holy book a few passages. I turned to them and marked them as he told me. He gave me the book, and said: 'If you will do just what the holy book says, Jesus will be your Saviour.'

" I send you the very same book with the passages marked, and I want you to do just as I did.

" The first passage was this: 'Search the Scriptures; for in them ye think ye have eternal life.' 'That means,' the missionary said, 'a careful study of the book will reveal Jesus.' I replied: 'I know that is so, for I have studied the book and found it full of Jesus.'

" The next passage was: 'Enter into thy closet, and when thou hast shut the door, pray to thy Father which is in secret, and thy Father which seeth in secret shall reward thee openly.' That means to ask

God to make plain the things which Jesus did and said.

"The next passage was : 'If any man willeth to do his will, he shall know of the doctrine.' That means, when you have found out what Jesus wants you to do, do it, and he will explain it.

"The last passage was : 'Come unto me, all ye that labor, and I will give you rest.' That means, in all your troubles or sorrows or duties, go to Jesus, and he will help you.

"I said : 'I will try it now ;' and I knelt down by the missionary's bed and repeated after him this prayer :

"'Dear Jesus, I have read about you in the holy book; I have heard about you from one of your servants; I have learned to love you; I want you to be my Saviour. I will become your disciple, and always serve and obey you.'

"While I was talking to Jesus I felt that some one was by my side; my heart grew warm and tender; it seemed to melt, and all desire for evil things was burned out, and love for the good took its place. I was filled with joy, and said : 'Glory to Jesus ! He is my friend.' I arose from my knees.

"The missionary said : 'I am happy. I am ready to go home now. I have a message I want you to

deliver.   The brilliant young literary man who
helped your brother write this catechism is my
brother.   I want you to send this letter to him inclosed in your next letter to your brother.   It is my
last word to any one in this world.'   He pointed to a
letter by my side on the table and rapidly sank
away.   He died about midnight.

"The day after we buried him I sat down to read
and study the catechism.   How different it seemed
to me now !   Jesus was my Saviour.   He would not
deceive me.   I started with him ; I studied the miracles he did.   I found nothing incredible.   If Jesus
could save me and cleanse my heart from sin and
make me a new man, as I knew he had, it was as wonderful as any thing written in the book.   If Jesus
gave to his disciples power to work miracles in his
name, I could believe that just as easy as if he had
done them himself.   I then tried to find out what
books Jesus had quoted as holy books.   I found him
quoting from the very books the critics were trying
hardest to destroy.   I found him relating as facts the
very marvels the critics ridiculed as fables or legends.
It did not take me very long to decide which to believe—Jesus or the critics.   I burned the catechism.
I found that the way to settle all these doubts is, first,
get Jesus in your heart as your Saviour, then take to

him in prayer the things in his word you cannot understand. It all becomes as clear as day. The more I study the holy book the more I believe it is the word of God."

***

CHAPTER VIII.

LETTER FROM NEW YORK.

"DEAR BROTHER: Your letter telling me about your very strange and wonderful experience made me very angry at first. After a little while my anger seemed so foolish that I chided myself for yielding to it. I said to myself: 'Your brother is an honest and sincere man. He is a man of great wisdom and learning. He is not one who would lightly discard his ancestral faith. It is impossible to believe that he could be deluded. It may be that what he says is true. As I too am an honest man I will do as he has done. I will investigate for myself.'

"I read the holy book carefully, just as you did, and it made exactly the same impression upon me that it did upon you. I purchased the little book called *The Life of Jesus in the Words of the Scriptures.* I read it so carefully and so frequently that I committed

it to memory.   At last I took the holy book you sent
me and went into my chamber and read over the passages, just as you did, and knelt down by my bed and
repeated the same prayer.   Jesus treated me just as
he did you.   My heart grew warm and the room became light and I heard music and I sang a Christian
hymn so loudly that some one knocked at the door
and said :

"'Are you sick or crazy? or what is the matter
with you?'

"I opened the door, and said : 'I am not crazy.   I
was a heathen a minute ago, but I prayed to Jesus
and he answered my prayer, and I am a Christian
now.   Do you love Jesus?'

"The man became angry and went away muttering:
'That's another of them gospel cranks!'

"I had decided that I would investigate this matter
for myself before I went near any of the critics.
The day Jesus became my friend I called upon the
young professor who had helped me prepare the catechism.   He recognized me at once.   He was very
pale and seemed greatly concerned.   I saw at once
that he had heard of his brother's death.   The first
question he asked me was :

"'Did you publish and distribute that catechism in
Japan?'

" I said : ' No !'

" 'Thank God !' he cried, with great emotion. ' I have not that sin to answer for.'

" He then told me that his twin brother had gone to Japan as a missionary, and although they differed in belief about the holy book he would have cut off his right hand before penning a word to hurt his brother or hinder his work.

" I then told him the wonderful story of your acquaintance with his brother—how he saved your life and taught you about Jesus, and thus prevented you from printing the catechism. The professor listened to me with the most intense emotion written in every feature. When I described the death-bed scene he broke down and cried as I never saw or heard a man cry. He sobbed as if his heart would break : ' O, Jack ! Dear old Jack ! How I have forgotten my promise to you. I wish I had died before stabbing your warm, loving heart with my wicked pen.'

" I was so overcome with the agony of his grief that I could not remain. I gave him the letter, and as I came away he was still sobbing and kissing the letter from his dead brother.

" I determined do a little missionary work myself. I called upon a number of the higher critics and told them my experience. They all listened very politely ; some with real interest, but most of them with a half-concealed sneer.

"I said: 'I understand you are all honest investigators. You seek only the right answer to all these questions. Will you now and here with me, a converted heathen, test the divinity of Jesus and his supernatural power by praying to him and asking him to make his own book clear and plain ?'

"Not one would for a single moment consider my proposition. They all wanted to discuss technicalities and niceties of language, and called my attention to the rules of criticism by which the holy book was to be tested before it could be accepted. Of course, I was ignorant of these things and could not express any opinion. I knew Jesus was divine, because he had saved me from my sins. I came back to that point, and insisted that, as the book offered a result to souls which was eminently desirable and beneficial, the only sensible and honest way was to accept the conditions the book enjoined and let it prove its own authority by accomplishing the result it professed to be able to do. If it were a great remedy for the diseases of the body, as it is for the sins of the soul, we could settle its claims very quickly by trying it. It would not be fair to take a prescription offered to heal a disease and criticise its grammar or spelling or writing, and reject it without trying the remedy, especially when countless millions have found it a never-failing and instantaneous relief from deadly disease. Not one single higher critic would agree to test the holy book by the standard of personal experience. I came from each believing him to be one of the class the apostle Peter had in mind when he wrote his second letter. He called them 'false prophets and false teachers, who privily bring in damnable heresies, even denying the Lord that bought them, and thus bring upon themselves swift destruction. They speak great swelling words of vanity. They are presumptuous, self-willed, and are not afraid to speak evil of dignities. Many shall follow their pernicious ways; by reason of whom the way of the truth shall be evil spoken of. Spots they are, and blemishes, sporting themselves with their own deceivings. They shall receive the reward of their own unrighteousness.'

"The day after I had visited the professor he came to see me. He did not seem like the same man. His eyes were bright; his face was illumined with a heavenly joy. I knew what it meant before he spoke. I exclaimed: 'Jesus is your friend. You have talked with him just as I did, and he has treated you just as he did me. He has saved you from your sins. Is it not so?' I grasped his hand, feeling in my soul

we were brothers in Christ.   He replied, with a sweetness and a joy that melted my heart :

"'Jesus has made it all plain to me.   He is my
friend.   I have given him my heart.   All my doubts
vanished when his peace and joy filled my soul.   I
came to tell you about it.   When you left me yesterday I was suffering the tortures of the damned.   I
have not had a moment's peace since I helped you
prepare that catechism.   I knew I had done the work
so well that if it were put in print in your country it
would be an overwhelming disaster to the religion of
my father and my brother.   I felt only grief for their
sakes ; but it utterly robbed me of my peace of mind.
When you came to see me, and told me that my
evil work had been prevented from accomplishing its
purpose, I was unable to conceal my joy.   But when
I found that my beloved brother's holy life had led
your brother to Christ, and that you had been led
to Christ in spite of all I had done to discredit
the religion of the Bible, I was convicted of sin
in the most overwhelming manner.   I, the son of
a Christian minister, a professor in a Christian uni-
versity, had used my vast learning and remarkable
ability to overthrow the cause of Christ.   Here was a
heathen man resisting my sophistry and, inspired by
my brother's self-denying and self-sacrificing faith,

finding Jesus as a Saviour. My sin against Christ seemed so deserving of eternal condemnation that I was overwhelmed with despair. The letter from my beloved Jack seemed the only ray of light amid the darkness that threatened to engulf me. Will he rebuke and denounce me, or will he help me to a hope that I may find forgiveness? I held his letter in my hand an hour, not daring to open it. It seemed as if the destiny of my immortal soul depended upon its contents. At last I was conscious that this tension of mind threatened loss of reason, and I opened the letter with a trembling hand. O! the joy it brought me no words can describe. Here it is:

" ' " DEAR TOM, BELOVED OLD PHARISEE: This is the last letter you will ever read from 'Jack the Prodigal.' I am no longer a prodigal, glory to Jesus! By the time you read this I will be at home in my Father's house. What a mercy that such a sinner as I was could be saved. I have found out why Jesus wanted me to come to Japan. I have been greatly blessed in my work. Many hundreds have been led to Christ by my words, but that has not been my most important work here. Jesus knew that you would be deceived into manufacturing that awful weapon for the overthrow of his religion in this land. He planned to have me here to destroy it before it accomplished any evil. I am so glad that I have saved you from the guilt of this crime. It is a comfort to me to know that when you found that your work might hurt me, your love for me prompted you to try to undo the evil. Ah, Tom! it was Jesus's loving heart you were stabbing as well as your Brother Jack's. What a wonderful book it was. I read it with terror and dread. I saw that the ingenuity and wonderful eloquence that for a moment made my own faith stagger would be overwhelming to our work here. I could not but feel a thrill of pride that my brother was such a marvelous genius, but you could well imagine the grief that followed when I saw you use your wonderful power to undermine the faith of your father's Saviour. O, Tom! my life is a cheap price to pay to stay your hand. If I could know that this message from your dying brother would lead you to Christ, I would die content. Remember father's dying message to me. O! what shall I say to him to-day when I meet him? The first question he will ask will be, ' Where's Tom ? ' I charge you as your brother, who would gladly give up heaven rather than have you lose it, don't cheat father and mother and Jack of your company when the family have their reunion in our home above. Dear Jesus, for father's sake save Tom. Father gave his life to thy service. I know him so well that if he finds, after saving others, any of his own should be lost, heaven would be hell. This is my last prayer, Dear Jesus, save Tom! Save Tom!

" ' " Good-bye, Tom, dear! Remember, you promised to meet us all in heaven! Don't forget! Your loving   JACK."

" 'You may be sure my heart went all to pieces. I could only drop upon my knees and cry and pray : "O Jesus, for father's sake, for Tom's sake, for thine own sake who died for me, save me!"

" 'Instantly my heart leaped with joy. The room seemed to be filled with heavenly light. I heard a sweet voice say, " Thy sins are forgiven thee." I have been as happy as a bird ever since. I resigned my position last night, and am now ready to go to Japan to take up Jack's work. I was fearful that all the reading and studying in the line of destructive criticism would leave my faith weak and unsatisfactory even in my new life of loving service. But I have given it the most thorough test. The presence of the divine Christ in my own heart is as great a miracle as the raising of Lazarus from the dead. All the supernatural of the Bible in the light of Jesus's presence is as clear as the noonday sun. What a purblind groveler I have been. I found upon close analysis that many years ago dear old Jack diagnosed himself and me with all the wonderful skill he afterward developed in his medical practice.

" ' He said : " Tom, you are trying to excuse your sins by picking flaws in the Bible ; I am excusing my sins by picking flaws in Christians. We are both in mighty mean business. You are a higher critic and I am a hypercritic. I am afraid both words could be spelled the same way and truly applied to us both— H-y-p-o-c-r-i-t-i-c." '

"You may be sure I was delighted that we were to have such a helper as this learned and brilliant man. We will start for Japan on the next steamer. Then for a life-time campaign. Our motto will be, ' *Japan for Jesus !* ' "

HOW SANTA CLAUS MADE ONE DOL-LAR HOLD OUT.

"MAMMA, may I send a Christmas box to a nero?"

"What is a nero, my dear?"

"A nero is a person who loves every body else better than he does his own wife and children. He wants to make all the world good and happy, and so he makes his own family mis'able by always being poor."

"You mean a hero instead of a nero, don't you, my dear?"

"Yes, I suppose I do; but if he gets my Christmas box he won't care whether I call him a nero or a hero. You see, the kind of a hero I mean doesn't work for a living like other people; he only preaches. He doesn't earn money like papa does; people gives him things to keep him from starving. I suppose it's grand to have a hero for a father, but I'd rather have an every-day sort of a man like my papa. You see, if papa was a hero he wouldn't have any money; we'd be poor, and people 'd send us cast-off clothing and cold victuals; and I'd rather have warm victuals and wear my own clothes before any one else does. Auntie read to me about some of these heroes away out West. They are missionaries. They are not real missionaries to the heathen, they are only missionaries to the Christians in the West. If they were real missionaries they would have plenty of clothes and food and good homes. Nobody ever begs for second-hand clothing for real missionaries. These missionaries hardly get enough to eat. They have to wear cheap second-hand clothing which people send them in barrels; lots of them live in houses made out of sod and dirt."

"My dear, who has been telling you all this nonsense?"

"It is not nonsense at all, but true sense. Auntie was reading it to me to-day out of the *Advocate*, and they don't put no nonsense in the *Advocate*. They are begging for money and clothing to help keep the heroes and their families from starving and freezing to death. The men do not have warm clothing; the women do not have nice dresses; and the little children do not have any toys or picture-books or dolls. I felt bad for the heroes; I felt badder for their wives; but I felt baddest of all for the children. Why, just think of it, no Christmas presents, no toys, and no dolls! It's just perfectly awful. So I said to auntie,

if my mamma will let me I will send a box to one
hero, and his family will have a Christmas what is a
Christmas. I would like to make believe I am Santa
Claus. I will—I will do without any Christmas gifts
myself and send them all the nice things Santa Claus
is going to get me."

"Well, my dear, I think you may send a box, but
Santa will hardly be likely to bring you enough to fill
a box."

"I will ask all the people I know to help me. The
things I beg you can put with the things Santa brings
me, and we will send them all together in one big box.
I guess I can make my old things do pretty well. My
old sled can be painted over, you know, and my dollie
can have a new head and a new body and some new
clothes, and I s'pose I can get along with her until
next Christmas."

And so it was settled. The little seven-year-old
girl was to play Santa Claus and do without any Christmas presents, and send a box to some misionary's
family out West. She was an industrious and per-
sistent little beggar. She asserted with a sweet will-
fulness that could not be resisted, that as every thing
she gave was to be new and nice, all other gifts must
be of the same kind. She would not accept any thing
that had been used.

12

"Just think of a minister hero getting up to preach with a bare-thread coat and a patch on; it would be too bad to send a hero-wife to meeting with a dress that had rust all over it just like an old tin kettle. I know I would cry if any one were to send me a dolly with the legs off and one eye punched out."

The way that Christmas box filled up was wonderful. The little Santa Claus was so delighted with her success that one day she said to her mother:

"Do you think you could spare me all night every Christmas? I'm thinking of being a real Santa Claus instead of a make-believe. It would be so nice to have a sleigh and some reindeers or a goat, and go around and give presents to poor children that don't get any!"

The mother smiled, and said:

"Then you are going to be like the heroes who think more of every body else than their own families, are you? Are you going to make other people happy, and your own poor mamma mis'able by running off and leaving her?"

"No, no! you old darling!" giving her a hug and a kiss. "I won't leave you only to make little short trips; or, O! if you only go with me we would have a bootiful time."

Many hundred miles away a missionary lived in a little box of a house that was an oven in the summer and a refrigerator in the winter. The minister and his wife, as soon as they were married, had gone to the far West, and had been working ever since upon the frontier in the little churches of the Western towns and circuits. The circuit upon which they were now stationed had six chapels. They were all little and cheap. The congregations were small and the people were all very poor. If all the salary promised was paid, the minister with a wife and three children could not have lived comfortably. But one half of it could not be paid. The crops had failed, the cold weather had killed much of the stock, business was dull, and times were very hard. Things looked desperate for the long bitter winter that was ahead. The stewards had been able to get together but one dollar, and to make it as easy to carry as possible they put it into one big silver dollar. The treasurer said:

"Brother, this is the best we can do; we do not know when we can get you another dollar. We think you had better go somewhere else and close up our churches."

They did not say just how he could move somewhere else with but one dollar. The minister was thin and white and looked as if he did not have enough to eat, but he was brave and true. The tears filled his eyes as he thought of his little family, but he said:

"No, brethren, I will not desert my post; God's

work must not stop. These six Methodist churches must not be closed. We will manage to get along somehow. God will take care of us."

He did not know just how, but as he rode home with but one dollar in his pocket, and knew that it was his only dollar, and the only one he would be likely to have for many a day, his faith did not waver. He sang over and over a verse of a little camp-meeting ballad:

> "O, do not be discouraged,
> For Jesus is your friend;
> He will give you grace to conquer,
> He will keep you to the end."

As he entered his little home his wife and three little ones, who had been long watching for him, pounced upon him and hugged and kissed him and shouted:

"Our dear papa has come; we will have a happy Christmas now."

It was Christmas eve. He had been away over one week in the distant part of his circuit. Sitting down by the little stove, he drew his wife to his side. Taking his boy of seven years upon one knee and his girl of five on the other, and putting the baby on his shoulder, he sang a simple little home song.

"Now, my darlings, you are in a happy good humor, and can stand a bit of bad news."

Seeing the startled look on each face, he said quickly:

"Here is all the money we have, and we can have no more for many days."

Opening his hand, he showed them the big silver dollar. Little Mary looked at it, and taking it up in her hands, said:

"How much money! It must be a hundred dollars."

"No, it ain't a hundred dollars, either," said Willie, "it's only one dollar. Do you call it news, papa, to tell us you are out of money? We know that all the time. Then looking at the silver piece, he said with a quivering lip, "If you have only one dollar we can't have any Christmas. What could Santa Claus do with one dollar? And if he were to take that dollar, what would we do for bread? Papa, why don't you get some business that will support your family, like other men?"

Two great tears gathered and trickled down his cheeks and splashed on his father's hand. Too brave to cry, he slipped down from his father's knee and ran to the window, and stood looking out into the thickly falling snow. The husband and wife looked into each other's eyes but a moment. Each saw a sorrow and pain too keen for words.

The minister said softly: "They offered to release me; they said they could not pay me any thing. I said we would not desert our post of duty. We would trust the Lord to take care of us. I am sorry for the children, it will be such a disappointment to them. This is the first Christmas they have ever missed."

Then gently stroking his wife's hair, already becoming sprinkled with gray, he said :

"I feel sorry for you, darling, my brave sweetheart. If it were not for you to help and encourage me, I am afraid I would have run like a coward long ago. You have never failed me. I have to cry all to myself when I think how poor and brave your life is. It almost breaks my heart when I remember that you refused an elegant home to share my humble little parsonage. But what would I have been without you? How could I get along without you?"

The brave little woman choked back a great sob that leaped from her heart and smiled dazzlingly upon the weary, white-faced man.

" My precious husband, you are my hero. I would not exchange my little home with you to share the palace of a king. I have not a regret for the past. I have not a thought of repining because of our privations. Love glorifies our poverty. We are dearer to each other because we have so little else to care for. But how pale and thin you are looking ! I fear this hard work and rough life will take you away from me. Then what would I do ? What would become of these? I will be happy, even if I am always poor and cold and hungry, if you are only spared to me."

She rested her head one moment upon his breast, and then said softly : "We will trust Him. He has never failed us yet. The one dollar with our Saviour is better than a million without him."

She hurried away to prepare the evening meal. The minister held the baby in his arms and sang as he rocked it :

> "O, do not be discouraged,
> For Jesus is your friend;
> He will give you grace to conquer,
> He will keep you to the end."

The little boy and girl stood by the window, hand in hand, and looked out into the blinding snow.

"It's all right, Willie. Santa Claus could never find his way out here in all this snow even if papa had plenty of money."

Willie looked his little sister in the face, and said :

"Will you tell if I say it?" and before she could reply he said :

"There ain't no Santa Claus ! "

"O, Willie!" was all she said, but it was the wail of a very sorrowful little heart. She stood and looked out into the snow and up through the gray clouds, and the great tears gathered and slipped down **over** her chubby cheeks in great splashes upon the window-sill.

" Come to supper, all ; we have bread and cheese and tea, and hugs and kisses for dessert."

The mother spoke with a cheery chirp to her voice. A bright smile was upon the face, from which every trace of tears had disappeared. Her eyes were as bright as her words were sweet and tender.

Little Mary said to her brother, who stood very penitently by her, as if sorry that he had hurt his little sister's heart but not sorry enough to confess it :

" Mamma has been talking with Jesus. That's what makes her so sweet and happy."

One warm mother-kiss dried the little wet eyes and stilled the little troubled heart.

" Let us play we are snow-bound travelers and provisions are scarce. We are snowed in and our rescuers are trying to dig through the great snow-bank. When they come they will bring meat and butter and milk and potatoes. Until they do come we will have to live on bread and cheese and tea. We will be brave and happy and make believe this is a great feast. The bread is sweet; mamma's hands filled it with love when she made it; the cheese is fresh, and the tea is warm. We will have two kinds of dessert. Hugs and kisses **from mamma**, and hugs and kisses from papa; you can have either or both. We will sing, ' Isn't this a dainty dish to set before a king?' I'd rather have bread and cheese with my darlings than roast turkey, cranberry sauce, and mince-pie all alone."

Cheated into hearty eating, the children laughed, and tried to count upon their fingers how many days it would take for their rescuers to dig through the great high, thick snow wall, and bring the meat and butter and milk and potatoes.

The father and mother nibbled at the bread, tasted a crumb of the cheese, and sipped at the weak tea. Both pretended not to be hungry and were deeply interested in the children's chatter. Innocent deceivers! Both knew that all the food in the house was upon the table and the children must first be satisfied. Both knew too well that one dollar would not go very far in buying even bread and cheese and tea for five.

The minister was in his study. The wife was sewing and trying to sing. Little Willie and his sister, hand in hand, stood by the mother's side. They had something important to say.

When the song reached a pause, Willie said: "Mamma, I ain't a Methodist any more. I'm a spek-tic now."

" What is a spektic, my dear ? "

" A spektic is a person who knows every thing and don't believe nothing. I mean he don't believe in the Bible and Methodism and Santa Claus."

" And so my little Willie don't believe in the Bible and Methodism and Santa Claus any more! Is my little girl a spektic, too ? "

" No, mamma, I'se no spektic! I believe in every thing mamma believes." And then bursting into a little camp-meeting ditty which she often sang, her sweet, clear voice filled the room as she poured forth the quaint melody :

> " I'se a Methodist bred
> And I'se a Methodist borned;
> And when I'se dead
> There's a Methodist gone. "

Before the mother could reply she was called to the study and the children were left alone.

" Willie, I'm ashamed of you ; to think you would go and become a spektic, and backslide and not be a Methodis' any more just because your father is poor and has only one dollar. I'd be a Methodis' if he hadn't one cent. What's dollars got to do with bein' a Methodis' ? I just know we are going to have Santa Claus come to our house. I asked Jesus to let either Santa or an angel bring us our Christmas presents, and I know he will, for he says, 'If two shall agree and ask, it shall be done.' You ain't agreed, and you don't count because you're a spektic; but mamma and me make two without you, and we have papa extra, so we've got Jesus sure. He never goes back on his word, mamma says, and mamma ought to know, for she's been acquainted with him ever since she was a little girl. And so when mamma read me what Jesus said, I just went into mamma's room and knelt down by her bed. You see, I thought as Jesus was so used to talking with her there, may be I could find him easier. I just 'minded him of what he'd said, and told him mamma and me made two and we was depending upon him. I told him I wasn't particular whether he sent an angel or Santa. If it was just the same to him, I'd a little rather have Santa. I was acquainted with him, and angels is strangers. You see I've knowed Santa nearly five years. Let's play church. You be the minister and I'll be the choir. You pray and I'll sing. Let's ask Jesus to be very sure and not forget our house."

"No!" said Willie, sturdily, "I can't pray any more. Spektics don't pray. I don't believe praying will do any good. Papa and mamma pray about it all time, and if Jesus won't hear them he won't hear us. I wonder if there is any Jesus!"

"Why, Willie, no Santa Claus and no Jesus! We might as well die and be done with it. I know there is a Jesus. I hear mamma sometimes when she goes into her chamber saying, 'Dear Jesus!' and when she comes out her eyes shine like stars, and sometimes she sings:

> "Dear Jesus, the very thought of thee
> With sweetness fills the breast."

And I ask her, 'Mother, did Jesus talk back to you?' And she says, 'Yes, my dear.' I'm going to pray myself if you won't."

Willie, at the very thought of his mother's sweet, trusting faith in Jesus, began to weaken a little. He said, hesitatingly:

"I won't kneel; spektics don't kneel. I will stand up. I won't pray, but I guess if you pray I can say amen."

Little Mary began:

"Dear Jesus, bless Willie. He is a spektic now. He ain't going to pray any more. He don't believe in Santa Claus. He don't know whether there is any Jesus or not, but I do, and mamma and papa does; make Willie a good Methodis' again. Why don't you say Amen, Willie?"

"Because you ain't done," said Willie; "and besides, you haven't said one word about the things I want. If you want me to say amen, you must pray for a sled and a pair of skates and a pair of mittens and a Christmas-tree; then I'll say amen. You might say something about a doll and a little play-kitchen for yourself, and something for baby and papa and mamma; then I'll say amen, loud and strong, to all your prayer; but you want to let my being a spektic alone."

Little Mary began:

" Dear Jesus, please send Santa Claus and a Christmas-tree."

" Amen," said Willie, in a whisper.

" Let him bring baby and mamma and papa something real nice."

" Amen," said Willie, in a low tone.

" Send Willie a new sled and a pair of skates and a pair of mittens."

" Amen," said Willie, with a strong Methodist accent.

" Send me a dollie and a little play-kitchen and a pair of mittens; that is, if you can make the dollar hold out after the other presents is got."

" Amen," said Willie, a little softer, as the big silver dollar began to grow smaller as the list of presents grew larger.

Mary stopped and said, " You pray now, Willie."

Willie began : " Dear Jesus, make me a good Methodist again ; I'm tired of being a spektic."

" Amen," said Mary, and the meeting was over.

" I feel better," said Mary ; " don't you, Willie ? "

" Yes," he said, frankly ; " but I wish I was sure Santa Claus would come."

The father and mother smiled and cried as they looked and listened through the partially opened door, but said nothing.

The children were all sound asleep and the minister and his wife were sitting together quiet and thoughtful. A strange noise was heard without. It sounded as if some strange animal was approaching the house. At last it stopped before the parsonage and a loud voice said, " Whoa ! "

" It must be Santa Claus," said the wife, and they hurried to the door.

It was one of the neighbors with two pair of oxen and a huge ox-cart whose wheels creaked and groaned as they crushed through the snow.

" Good-evening, or rather good-morning, dominie. This ye're ain't no sleigh and reindeer party, and I am a pretty tough looking Santa Claus. I look more like old Nick than Saint Nick, but I've brought you your Christmas present. It came to-day, and the station man down at the railroad wanted me to bring it around. All expenses is paid, and I don't charge nothing for my services. Lend a hand and we'll get it in the house. It's a whopper, I tell ye!"

It was hard work to get it in the house. It was large and heavy and seemed almost to fill the little room. The lid was soon off. The most wonderful Christmas box a poor missionary ever received dazzled their eyes. It was wonderful how much even so large a box could hold. There was a full suit for the minister—overcoat, gloves, and great fur riding-cap. There were beautiful dresses for the minister's wife —winter cloak, gloves, shoes, stockings, warm, fine underwear, and a white fleecy hood; a full suit for the boy—cap, overcoat, tippet, mittens, and rubber boots; warm and beautiful dresses for little Mary— heavy cloak, mittens, shoes and stockings, and the cutest little muff and tippet. Baby was not forgotten. He received soft flannels and dresses and the daintiest baby shoes you ever saw. After all these had been taken out the house looked like a dry-goods emporium fitted out for the holidays. And still the wonderful box was half full. Now forth came a sled, a pair of skates, a beautiful doll, and a charming play-kitchen. In the very bottom was a little Christmas-tree with candles, stars, crowns, and angels. Underneath the tree was a huge package of candies, nuts, and oranges.

The minister stopped to pray two or three times before he emptied the box, and finally began to sing:

"O, do not be discouraged,
For Jesus is your friend;
He will give you grace to conquer,
He will keep you to the end."

Just before daylight all the wonderful presents were in full view, the Christmas-tree was set up, and the candles lighted. The children were awakened by hearing the doxology sung as if a camp-meeting was going on.

Willie was wild with delight. Little Mary hardly seemed surprised at all. She went around patting each present lovingly, and said:

"Zactly right. I knew there was a Jesus. I knew he would send Santa Claus or an angel, one of the two; but how did they ever make the dollar hold out?"

The most wonderful part of this story is that every thing fitted as if it had been made to order. Little Mary said "she 'sposed old Santa Claus took their measure when they were all asleep. The minister found in the pocket of his coat a letter. It said:

"I am a crusty old batchelor who never had a wife or a child. I don't take much stock in the ordinary Santa

Claus, but when a golden-haired fairy plays the game I acknowledge myself beaten and surrender at once. I send my Christmas gift in the form you will appreciate most."

Ten crisp ten-dollar bills were inclosed.

Little Mary put her hands into her muff to see how warm and nice it was. She found a letter. It said:

"Dear hero friends, please accept this Christmas box from a little girl Santa Claus."

The tiny picture of a golden-haired, rosy-cheeked, seven-year-old girl, cased in a little silver frame, dropped to the floor.

Little Mary picked it up, and said:

"Jesus did not send Santa Claus; he sent an angel instead, and that's how the dollar held out."

Willie took the picture, and said:

"I mean to marry this Santa Claus, so that when I preach like papa does I will have a Santa Claus to live with me all the time, like papa does." With a kiss upon his mamma's cheek, he whispered: "I ain't no spektic now. I'm a good Methodist again, and I'm going to try and never backslide no more."

13

THE TALE A LAMP-POST TOLD ME.

———•———

" WOULD you like to hear a sermon, dominie?"
I was alone upon a street corner. The
voice startled me. I could see no one. I was about
to disbelieve my ears when I heard a strange laugh.
The "ha-ha" sounded like taps upon a window-pane.
I looked in the direction from which the laugh came
and saw a lamp-post, that was all; but it was the
strangest lamp-post you ever heard of. It had the
queerest looking face, which seemed to peep out of
the glass lantern as out of a huge cap. The light had
turned to an eye that fairly twinkled with merriment
at my surprise and wonder. It was New Year's day.
I had made but four calls. I had sipped lemonade
twice and coffee once. I tried to think which had
tasted like—

"Would you like to hear a sermon, dominie?" the
voice spoke again, interrupting my troubled thoughts.

It was the lamp-post speaking. I was sober. Before I could speak the lamp-post laughed again until
its glass cap rattled as if it would break.

"Don't be alarmed, dominie. You preach yourself, and perhaps you would rather hear a story than
a sermon. I shouldn't wonder if your people felt the
same way sometimes. I could tell many a tale. I
see many queer and funny sights; I hear many sad
and terrible things as I stand here night after night
looking and listening. I've wanted to talk with
somebody for a long time; I've tried many times.
But when once my voice was heard the man ran for
life. I never tried to speak to a woman, because I
can't run away."

That peculiar, weird laugh fairly gave my blood a
chill as the glass cap rattled as if it would break. I
rubbed my eyes in surprise. It seemed as if the arms
which lamp-posts generally carry akimbo were pressing its sides as it swayed to and fro in rollicking
laughter.

"I feel quite confidential with you now since I
have decided to preach. I am one of the cloth, you
know. If you listen to me I will give you material
enough for a dozen sermons. I can tell you tales that
will crack your sides with laughter or break your
heart with pity and grief."

Just then a dirty, ragged wretch staggered against
me heavily.

"Beg your pardon, boss (hic). I've been makin'

New Year's calls (hic). I've swore off six times to-day, 'm goin' t' swear off 'gin (hic) to-night."

He staggered off up the street shivering, swearing, and singing. I thought I heard the lamp-post sigh. When it spoke again all the merry banter was gone. The voice was soft and sad like the moaning of the wind sweeping down the street. Its single eye flickered and grew dim as if full of tears. I was first chilled and then melted as I listened, like one in a dream.

"Poor Harry!" it said, "you don't know him. I do. I've known him a long time. I've tried to talk to him. To hear a lamp-post speak and see it smile and wink at him made him think the terrible delirium was coming again. He would run as if the demons were after him the moment I began.

"When I first saw him he was as clean and spruce a young fellow as ever walked these streets. He was a fresh young country boy, with clear eyes and blooming cheeks. It made my heart ache to see him. I had seen so many just like him come to the city only to be ruined that I feared for him. I called him my country boy, and always watched for him as the whistle blew. He would stride along with a boyish, swinging walk, as if he were in a hurry to drive home the cows at milking time. The first

time I saw him dressed up I was frightened enough
to cry.   You never saw a lamp-post cry, did you ?   I
shed one tear, and that almost put my one eye out.   I
was vexed enough to give myself a good shaking.   I
believe I did try, but I made such comical work of
it that I had to laugh, and cracked one pane of my
glass cap.   I saw by the curl of hair pomaded down
upon his forehead and the bright necktie, new
gloves, and natty cane that he was going to see his
girl.   I muttered to myself : ' What a fool you are
making of yourself ; he has found a sweetheart, and
that is always an anchor to a young man if she is the
right kind.   I know she is.   A boy with a face and
laugh like his will fall in love with a girl like his
sweet, pure sister.'

"While I was talking to myself he was standing
close by my side, gently rapping me with his little
cane and softly whistling.   He suddenly looked up
and started as he saw my face.

"'I declare,' said he, 'I do believe that this lamp-
post is trying to get up a flirtation with me.'   Then,
with a merry smile and low bow he laughed, ' It's no
use, old lady, I have one girl.'   I blushed until the
glass in my cap became almost a ruby red.

"I watched him every night now as he came
from work, and then, dressed in his Sunday suit,

would hurry by.   To my great joy she was with him
one night.   They had been to church.   She was hum-
ming a hymn.   They stopped right here by me to
chat a little while.   I never wanted to bend so badly
in my life.   I wanted to stoop and see her face.   She
started and clung a little closer to him as she said :
'Harry, I do believe that lamp-post bent a little bit.'

"'Nonsense,' he laughingly replied, as he clasped
her hand.   Then a little more seriously, he said : 'Do
you know, Maud, I have imagined I have heard this
same lamp-post try to speak to me ?   It frightened
me at first, but now it seems like an old friend.'

"She looked me in the face and then cried with real
fear, 'O, Harry, look!   The lamp-post has a face ; its
light looks like an eye.'   I had been so anxious to see
her that when she did look at me I really stared at her.
I ought not to have done it.   I don't wonder she was
frightened.   That one glance satisfied me, and I looked
another way as he put his arm around her.   She hid
her face on his shoulder and I think he kissed her.
At any rate, she was blushing when I looked again.
She was a sweet, pure, young girl, just such a one as
my country boy's mother or sister would have picked
out for him.   I tried to look like any other lamp-post
as they started to go away.   She threw me a kiss as she
said, 'Good-night, old lamp-post.   Don't tell any body,

please.' I was really ashamed my arms were so stiff I
could not throw her a kiss in return. They came by
every night now, and always stopped near me for a
little chat. I soon learned all about them. She was
a shop-girl earning a scanty pittance which barely en-
abled her to live. Life was an endless battle for bread
and shelter and clothing, unrelieved by scarce a gleam
of sunshine until he came. They were to be married
soon and struggle along together. With brave hearts
they planned to deny themselves every possible thing,
that their scanty earnings might furnish their cosy
little nest of two rooms. Their wedding eve they
passed me going to the minister's and then to their
little home. They did not notice me this time. They
only had eyes for each other I lost sight of them
for many months. One night a man, staggering along,
stumbled and threw his arms around me to keep from
falling. As he stood half clinging and half leaning,
trying to steady himself, he muttered :

" ' I believe this is my very old friend, the lamp-
post. Glad to see you, old fellow ; 'f 't hadn't been
for you I'd had a bad tumble ; one good turn d'serves
another ; 'f ever you need a friend, just send for me.'

" I was so startled by the change in my country boy
that I trembled until I broke every glass in my cap ;
a tear I could not stop blinded my eye, and a gust of

wind coming along just then put it clear out.   The
policeman on that beat said as he rapped me with his
night-stick, 'Out for the first time in five years.'

"That saloon at the corner became his loafing-place
every night.   One night he was thrown out into the
street unable to walk.   He curled up against me in a
drunken sleep.   She found him here.   What a change
the few months had wrought!   She was shabbily and
thinly dressed.   Wan and gaunt looking, with great
black rings around her eyes, she looked more like a
ghost than a creature of flesh and blood.   The policeman helped her get him on his feet, and then leaning
upon her he shambled out of sight.   Every night now
she came after him and stood here right by me waiting to help him home.   One night--I wish I could
forget it—he was quarrelsome.   He resented her spy-
ing and hanging around, and after working himself
into a fury he struck her in the face with his clenched
fist.   She fell against me, and that sharp corner there
cut a fearful gash in her face.   I believe the blood is
there yet.   Sobered by the result of his wicked blow,
he picked her up and carried her home.   The next
time I saw her she came out of that saloon too drunk
to walk, and clung to me until the policeman dragged
her away and threw her into the patrol-wagon and
took her to the station-house.   I heard she had been

sent to the island for three months. My heart is iron,
but it was broken that night. I loved Harry and
Maud—"

The voice ceased. I looked at the lamp-post.
There was no face. The gas flickered and sputtered.
Had I been dreaming? As I passed to my home the
story of these two lives was as real to me as if I had
always known them.

*   *   *   *   *   *

I was in my church at a joyous festal occasion.
Flowers, music, and bright faces made the hour one of
surpassing delight. I was summoned to a side room
by the bustling sexton. " A couple to be married,
dominie," he whispered with a smile. As he introduced me he said : " The dominie is enjoying a wel-
come reception from his church. He is in a capital
state of mind to marry people. You've hit him at
the right time." When we were alone the man said :
" We are not here to get married ; we are married. I
have brought you my wife to have her sign the
pledge." I looked at her in surprise. She was a
comely young woman, neatly, although very poorly,
dressed. She returned my glance with defiance as she
turned upon her husband, saying, " If I sign the pledge
you've got to promise you'll not beat me. You taught
me to drink and now beat me because I won't stop."

Sullenly the man told his story. He had been in-
temperate. He had abused his wife until, in desper-
ation, she had taken to drink. When he learned that
his wife, too, was a drunkard he had reformed, but
had tried in vain to induce her to give up the drink.
She had been arrested a score of times. She had
been to Blackwell's Island twice.

"We were at your church last night and determined to try and begin a new life. Will you not
write a pledge for both of us ?"

I drew up a pledge.; they signed it. We prayed
together, and they passed out. I looked at the sig-
natures. I read, " Harry and Maud ———." The next
day I called at the address given me. They had
moved, no one knew where.

*   *   *   *   *   *

A biting December day in holiday week I received a note saying a dying woman wished to see me.
I called immediately. I was directed to a back room
upon the top floor of a large, cheap tenement-house.
When I knocked, a faint voice said, "Come!"

I entered. A woman was lying upon a pallet of
straw upon the floor. She was emaciated to a
shadow. Her long black hair hung about her thin
white face, in which a pair of black eyes fairly
gleamed like the eyes of a famished wolf. Around

her shoulders was but a cotton night-dress. In a tiny
stove a handful of coals faintly glowed. I was chilled
to the bone as I sat with my great ulster overcoat on.
I said, " Are you alone ? " She whispered, " Yes."

" Have you any thing to eat ? "

She pointed to a cracker and a half cup of cold
tea.

" Is that all ? " I asked.

She nodded. " He has not been here all day. He
is drinking again. I kept the pledge you gave me.
God has helped me. He is going to take me home
soon. I am glad."

The black eyes looked up through the grimy ceil-
ing, through an open gate, and saw warmth and food
and love, and smiled. As she smiled, the hungry
look faded out of her eyes and they shone with tears.
We made her comfortable for a few days and then
laid her away to rest. A simple stone marks the
spot. It bears the name of Maud ——.

  *   *   *   *   *   *

I was passing up the street. A horse and wagon
dashed along at a fearful rate. The drunken man in
the wagon was unable to control or guide the frightened beast. They turned the corner and came down
in a heap together. The wagon had been dashed
against a lamp-post, snapping the iron shaft off close

with the ground. The man was dead. The lamp-post lay across his mangled face. As I lifted the lamp-post from the body I thought I heard it sigh and felt it tremble. It was my old friend.

The dead man was Harry ——.

www.ingramcontent.com/pod-product-compliance
Lightning Source LLC
Chambersburg PA
CBHW030829020726
47499CB00006B/2132